THE MIRACLE OF JOIE

A SWEETHART'S CAFE ROMANCE CHRISTMAS

BETSY LOVE

Dedicated to the people in my life who bring me Joy. I'd list you, but that would take too many pages. You know who you are.

CHAPTER ONE

Some secrets Santa simply could not be trusted with. His duties lie in fulfilling the expectations of millions of children all over the world. Only Mrs. Claus could fulfill special miracles found in the hearts of the purest children. This was one of those special letters.

Deer Mrs. Claus,

Santa probly gits lots of letters and I wantd to make shur mine didnt git lost. I no hes reely buzi with ordering his elfs around and gitting them to make mor toys cuz thers lots mor kids arownd nowadays. So I am riting to you cuz I know you'll make sure to help me with my Christmas wish.

I dont want a toy this year. I want sumthing reely speshul, and its not for me, but it kind ov is. It's for my dad. He needs a wife and that way I get a mommy.

He didnt get any presents for two hole years. Thats cuz my mommy and I wur in a bad car acsident. Mommy died and Im stuk in a wheelchar. Daddy is so sad that he forgets Christmas. We didnt even put up the Christmas tree last year and weer not gonna put up one this year ether. And so I think thats why Santa wont bring anething. And I was in the hospital the yar befor that.

Grammy got me some stuff, but Daddy didnt want anithing. So she gav him a credit card thing. I saw it last week. Its steel in his walet. Aniway, I know that yul make sure to help Daddy get a wif. I think he prefurs ladis with blond hair and blu iyes, but wel tak anione as long as shes nis and doznt run wen she sees me.

Your frend,

Emily

PS. My dog died, too. So if my new mommy has one that wud be grat. Unless its a litl one. They bark to much.

Mrs. Claus smiled. She knew just the right elf for the job! Joie Noel...but here in North Pole Kingdom, everyone calls her Joy, because that's who she is.

CHAPTER TWO

Matthew Adam's radio sat silent, void of the Christmas music ringing through the airwaves, just as it had been for the past two years. Even during the year, Matthew rarely turned it on. His wife had loved listening to music, especially this time of year. The woman had been crazy about the season, often scolding him for not getting into the spirit of it all. Flipping radio stations was something Cadence liked to do. Not Matt. His business took priority, and when the weather was good, his boys stayed later making up for rainy days.

As he sped his truck toward the sleepy town of Miracle, Texas, the pine trees zipped by in an endless sea of dark green, the murky dusk deepened the grieving in his heart. Even the slight flush of pink from the fading sunset casting a sheen against the wet asphalt did little to bring him joy.

Matt rounded the bend where his wife had taken her final breath and left his daughter, Emily, bound to a wheelchair for the rest of her life. He gripped the steering wheel tighter. If only Cadence had waited until morning to run her errand.... She never listened to him. Worse still, if Laura Milo hadn't been texting and driving, his wife would still be alive. Sadness threatened to overwhelm; instead he focused on his anger. Her penalty and fines would never compensate for her horrid choice. No message justified being so stupid.

He'd give anything for Cadence to not listen to him one more time and set about doing things her own way.

Mrs. Milo had stolen everything from him.

He hit the high beams after a semi passed and tried to ignore the ditch where her car had rolled. Once he got to the other side of the fatal spot, a huge gray critter with way too many eyes reflected back at him. Matt slammed on the brakes. The tires screeched to a halt in front of an animal. Hands shaking, he pulled to the side of the road and threw on his hazards. With a well-chosen swear word, he exited the truck. The chill in the air nearly sucked his breath away. His truck headlights glowing off the back of all those retinas sent the heebie-jeebies crawling up his spine like a jumping wall spider.

Danged opossums! This mama was either dead or playing dead. Sometimes it was hard to tell. Either way, he couldn't leave them here in the middle of the road to get hit. He grabbed the lifeless critter by the tail and dragged it across the road. Several of the babies hissed at him, baring their teeth. One even snapped at him.

Matt yanked his hand back. No need to get rabies. Six of the vermin clung to the mama's dead body. Cadence would have applauded his kindness at saving defenseless creatures. He went back to his truck and tried to locate something to wrap the babies in. Nothing.

With a heavy sigh, he pulled off his shirt, laid it at the side of the road, and pried the young'uns off the mama's back. The last one, nearest the mama's head, did not want to let go of her fur. It hissed and bared its teeth. He supposed that's the way it was with some of the chillins, bite and hiss at the hand that brings ya to safety. These little ones would miss their mama for sure.

Matt grabbed the cuff of his shirt, and stuffed his hand inside, then gently grabbed the baby opossum by the scruff of its neck and tucked it inside the long sleeve. The others had nestled down, probably felt kind of like the warmth of their mama.

Shivering, Matt picked up the bundle and set them on the back seat. After climbing inside his truck, he turned up the heat. Then leaning his head back against the rest, he let out a breath. Once he put his car in drive, he headed off down the road to home.

"Do you think perhaps your wife wants to tell you that you're doing a good job taking care of your daughter, by setting those babies in the middle of the road for you? It might just be a message from the other side."

Surprised, Matt jerked the wheel of his car, swerved off the road and headed down an embankment before he slammed on his breaks, bringing his vehicle to a stop. His heart pounded.

The bundle on the back seat landed with a thunk on the floor. Six little howlers set up a commotion.

Matt turned and searched the back seat. "Who said that?"

Suddenly, lights flashed behind him. A highway patrol car pulled off the road slightly up the embankment from him. The flashlight bounced in the rearview mirror as the officer descended the hill.

Rolling down the window, the cold night air prickled his bared arms in spite of the warmth inside the truck.

"Is everything all right?" The officer shined his light inside. The beam rested on the bottle of MARTINELLI's, the cap had come off, and the inside of the car reeked of apple cider.

"I'm...I'm fine." Matt stumbled over his words. His heart had sped up with the appearance of the patrolman.

"Step out of your vehicle." The officer backed up to allow Matt to open his door.

Matt left the warmth and stepped into the frigid night. "I haven't been drinking. That's a non-alcoholic beverage." Matt pointed back inside the truck where the bottle rested.

"I'd still like to run a sobriety test." His name badge read Goodman.

Matt took a deep breath. "I was just getting some baby opossums off the road. Their mama was dead, and I didn't want the little ones to get hit by oncoming traffic."

"How did you end up down here?" Officer Goodman asked.

Matt didn't dare tell him he was hearing voices, or he'd do more than take a breathalyzer test. "The critters started making noises, I looked back to check on them. I know, it was stupid to take my eyes off the road." Matt wished he'd shine his flashlight anywhere but his face. It made it hard to see the officer.

"Where are they now?" Skepticism came thickly in his voice.

"I think they rolled under my seat." Matt started to reach for the handle of the back door.

Officer Goodman pulled his gun. "Put your hands up."

Matt had never stared down the barrel of a gun before. If his heart was pounding hard previous to the policeman's appearance, for sure he could see it pulsing through his thin undershirt. "Sorry." He stepped back.

The officer opened the back door, keeping his piece aimed at Matt. After doing a thorough search of the back seat, he reached under the driver's side seat and pulled the flannel shirt out. "I guess you were right." He held up the writhing material, the orneriest critter stuck its head out of the sleeve and hissed. Goodman dropped the shirt. "If you'd like, I'll take these to the animal shelter."

Matt wrapped his arms around himself and shivered. "That... would be...great." His chattering teeth made it hard to speak.

After his breathalyzer came back zero percent alcohol, Officer Goodman motioned to the car. "Go on, get back in. I'll send a tow truck to pull you out of the ditch."

"Thanks." Matt got in, closed the door and rolled up the window. He started the engine and blasted the heater as high as it would go. Matt had heard a voice as plain as day, as if someone sat in the front seat. But there'd been no one there. He pressed his hands into his eyes. Please, don't go to that dark place. Emily needed him.

CHAPTER
THREE

Joie hadn't meant to frighten Matt so badly that he had sent his truck careening over the edge. Wow, she didn't even realize she'd been invisible. Then again, if he'd seen her in her elf form, he might have been even more frightened. She'd just meant to whisper in his ear. Sometimes Joie forgot how loud her voice could be. When she got excited, she simply couldn't help it.

Biting her lower lip, she stood outside the passenger door. There had to be a better way to introduce herself and explain her mission. Around her wrist hung the miracle bracelet Mrs. Claus had given her. Five charms – a snowman, ice skates, an angel, and a miniature snow globe, and a candy cane hung from the silver links. She stroked the snowman. Was this a good time to use one of the miracles enveloped by the charm? No, it didn't have the warmth it did when Mrs. Claus had placed it on the bracelet. Mrs. Claus told Joie she'd know when the time was right. She put on her loveliest smile and tapped on the passenger side window.

Matt jumped. Blow Pops, that man was jittery. Maybe he hit his head when he went careening down the embankment.

Joie opened the door and bounded up into the massive truck. She settled into the soft bucket seats and smiled as sweetly as she could. "I'm sorry I scared you."

"Where did you come from?" Matthew gripped the handle as if he might make a dash into the woods.

"Oh, north of here a ways." She pointed with her thumb as if she hitchhiked along the road behind her.

"Where are your mom and dad?" His expression looked so concerned. That was awfully nice of him. She'd have to make sure that his new wife matched how kind and sweet he was.

Ignoring his question, she broadened her smile, hoping he'd loosen up a little. "I'm here to help you."

He fiddled with the door handle. "We need to find your parents. Where are they?"

"Don't worry; Kris and Laila know where I am. And they're not really my parents, but they take care of all the residents in NPK." Joie adjusted her bracelet, several of the charms holding the miracles tinkled together. Was she really the right elf for the job? She was certainly making a mess of this, and she'd hardly said anything at all. No, she couldn't go back, not when she'd just gotten here. Maybe beating around the igloo wasn't the best idea. Perhaps the straight peppermint stick approach would work best.

Joie cleared her throat. "I'm sorry. I've gotten off to a bad start." She held out her hand. "My name's Joie Noel. It's French for Joy. And of course, Noel means Christmas. I'm an elf who's come in answer to Emily's letter to Mrs. Claus."

"Look, little girl–"

"Joie, and I'm actually coming up on my twenty sixth year. I was born on Christmas Day. Do you know how wonderful it is to share a birthday with the Christ child?" She continued to fidget with the bracelet.

"Did Craig put you up to this?"

"Oh, no. Craig is at home right now with his kids. They're decorating the tree. Olivia is cooking up some mighty fine wassail." Joie smacked her lips. While she guessed that Olivia was quite adept in the kitchen, no one made wassail like Mrs. Claus.

Matthew withdrew his cell phone and selected a number from his contact list. Joie patiently waited for him to verify her information on the Layton family. "Hey, Craig. What are y'all up to tonight?"

"Just putting up the tree." Joie could easily hear Craig on the other end. She could also hear the excitement of the children in the background along with "Jolly Old St. Nicolaus" playing on the radio, the children singing along at the top of their lungs. "You should stop by for some wassail. Bring Emily. The girls would love it."

Joie couldn't help but grin.

Matthew eyed Joie. "Do you know a girl named Joie?"

"You on a date?" Incredulity filled Craig's voice. "That would certainly be a miracle."

"No, I'm not on a date." Matthew frowned at Joie. "I've picked up an eight or nine-year old hitchhiker whose parents should be shot for allowing her out by herself."

"You don't sound so good," Craig said, concern thick in his voice. "You haven't been drinking, have you? You're not hallucinating are you?"

"No. I'm fine. See you Monday." Shaking his head, Matthew clicked the end button and turned back to Joie. "Well, Miss Noel. I'm going to take you to the sheriff's office as soon as the tow truck arrives. I hope they press charges against your parents."

Joie bit her lip. This was not going as planned.

CHAPTER
FOUR

Matthew turned back to his steering wheel and tapped his thumbs against the metal, wishing the tow truck would hurry and show up. He could have sworn he heard her voice inside his truck earlier. But that couldn't have been since she'd been outside his truck. He eyed the child sitting in the front seat. Could she have snuck out when he was talking to the cop?

Joie kept playing with the bracelet around her wrist, fingering each charm. She must be cold in her thin red sweater. Her red and white plaid skirt fell just below her knees. Her feet clad in black shoes with silver buckles were crossed primly at the ankles. "So, I understand this is the area where your wife died."

How did she know that? He did not want to talk about Cadence.

Joie patted his hand. "It's hard to lose someone close to you."

Something about the tone of her voice sounded grown-up and sympathetic, not at all like the child she appeared to be.

"Children are actually quite resilient." Joie continued, her smile warming the inside of the car. This little girl had quite a persona about her. Her blue eyes held a depth of sincerity. He'd probably be more freaked out except for the feelings of love and compassion filling the car.

"That's what they say." Matt found himself smiling in spite of his predicament.

Joie chuckled. "There now, see that wasn't so hard."

"What?" Matt drew his brows together.

"Smiling." Her eyes lit with pleasure. "I'll bet you don't drop many of those."

"It's been a hard couple of years. Hardest on Emily." He hadn't meant to open up. Something magical was happening in the car. His phone call with Craig had left him unsettled. At first, all he'd wanted to do was to get her out of his truck, but now he rather liked the child. Emily might enjoy having a playmate. He'd have to find her parents and arrange a play date.

Joie put her hand on Matthew's arm. "Since the accident left her paralyzed, she's had a hard time adjusting, hasn't she?" The warmth of her tiny hand surprised him, especially since she wasn't wearing a jacket and she hadn't been sitting in the car long enough for the heater to make a difference. He was still feeling the effects of the cold.

"How do you know all this?" He drew his arm away from her.

"I told you, I'm an elf. I've come to help you find a wife." She grinned at him.

"Now don't start that again. We all know that elves are pretend and the only one I indulge in is the one sitting on my shelf."

"I'm sure Santa has more elves on shelves than you have shelves for elves." Joie giggled. "That was funny, huh? Santa uses that phrase all the time. It gets funnier every time he says it."

"Well, the one on my shelf is making sure my daughter stays out of trouble." Matt did not appreciate her humor.

Joie burst out laughing. "Your sweet Emily getting into trouble?" She shook her head. "That child doesn't have a sour bone in her body. From the tip of her toes all the way up to the top of her head, that child is pure delight, all gumdrops and peppermint sticks." Joie put her hands on her hips. "And honestly, how much trouble can a child in a wheelchair get into?"

"Oh, plenty." Matt pulled his eyebrows together. How had this little girl gotten him to talk so freely? Better yet, how did she know so much about his family? He looked up and saw the flashing yellow lights of the tow truck. At last! Now he could drop this little girl off at the station, and they could find her family.

"Stay right here." Matt got out of the truck as the driver pulled his tow truck to the edge of the embankment.

"Oh, hey Matt." Steve's flashlight shined in Matt's face as the driver traversed the embankment. "Whaterya doing down here?"

"Long story involving baby opossums."

"You swerve to miss em?" He scratched his head as he walked around Matt's truck.

"Yeah, their mama was dead. I couldn't leave her in the middle of the road. Never put those rascals in your shirt." Matt rubbed his arms, his skin prickling with goose bumps.

"Ain't you got a jacket?"

"Was wearing flannel."

"C'mon, I've got something you can wear. It's probly a might too big, but at least it'll keep ya warm." Steve headed back to his truck.

Matt followed Steve up the side of the ditch.

Steve rummaged in the back seat of his tow truck before handing Matt a jacket. "Here ya go."

"Thanks." Matt shrugged into the huge mass of fleece and fur.

"You better stay up here while I get your truck hooked up to the winch." Steve climbed into the cab of his truck.

He couldn't let Steve pull his truck out with Joie still in the front seat. He tapped on the window for the driver to roll it down. "Wait a minute. I need to get Joie out."

"Joie?"

He wasn't even sure how he was going to explain his little hitchhiker. "My passenger. I found her on the side of the road. I was going to take her to the police station, but I ended up in the ditch."

“Well, you go get her, and I’ll turn my truck around.” Steve cranked the window back up.

Matt hurried back down the hill and climbed inside his truck. “You can’t sit in here while he pulls my truck out of the–”

The inside of the truck was empty. He hadn’t meant to scare her off.

CHAPTER FIVE

Worried that Emily might be frightened by her appearance like her father had been, Joie stayed invisible and watched the little girl sitting at her desk. Emily had organized all her colors forming a rainbow. Red crayon on the right followed by the orange, all the way to the left where she ended with purple, just like a prism. When Joie was little, Pepper Minstix had explained in painting class how the colors absorbed light and made a picture take on certain tones. Is that what she called it? Or was it shades? She could never remember which one was which. Or maybe it was hues. Whatever it was called, Joie loved putting them together in artistic ways. She was going to get along great with Emily.

Picking up the middle crayon, Emily carefully drew a Christmas tree, leaving plenty of open areas for the ornaments. With a red one, she sketched in boxes for the presents. She gave a little sigh. "I hope Santa brings my special present."

"Oh, he will."

Emily jumped, knocking her perfect arrangement of crayons onto the floor. "Who said that?"

Jujubes, she'd done it again. Nothing to do but show herself to the little girl. She slowly materialized and put on her happiest face so as not to further frighten the child.

Emily gasped. “You’re an elf!”

“Indeed I am.” Joie gave a little curtsy.

“You’re from the North Pole.” With a concerned pull of her eyebrows, Emily narrowed her eyes. “Did Mrs. Claus send you? Cuz you know, I did write that letter to her.”

“Yes, she did.” Joie grinned at the darling little girl. “I’m Joie Noel. Pleased to meet you.”

“Oh, I just knew it. I knew Mrs. Claus would help.” Emily bounced in her wheelchair, making the table shake where the rest of her crayons rolled out of place. She made a mad grab for them. The purple one rolled onto the floor along with the green one.

“I’ll get those for you.” Joie scooped the crayons up and plopped them on the table, making the others roll, completely disorganizing the pattern. Joie arranged them exactly the way Emily liked them. “There you go, perfect as pie.”

“You’re here to help my daddy find a wife and a new mommy for me.” She clasped her hands over her drawing. “If you can do that, I don’t care if you mess up my whole room.”

“Oh, I wouldn’t want to do that.”

“Who’s going to be my new mommy?” Emily asked.

Joie pulled up a chair and sat at the table with Emily. “I don’t know yet, but I need your help to make a plan.”

Emily plopped her elbows on the table and rested her chin in her upturned hands. “Daddy hasn’t had very many dates. I guess it’s ‘cuz of me. They probably think I’m too much trouble.”

“You? Trouble?” Joie patted Emily’s arm. “You are as nice and sweet and cute as they come. We need to find someone who is worthy to be your mama.”

Emily crossed her arms and put her head down. “They see my face and get scared.”

“Of one little scar?” Joie pushed Emily’s hair behind her ear. “Besides, you can’t even see it when your hair is down. People can be so insensitive sometimes. Anyone can see that you'd make the best daughter ever."

"I guess. I am a super smart girl. And I'm never mean. And I always do what my dad asks."

Joie nodded. "Yes, you are an awesome girl." She couldn't let Emily have a new mom who didn't like her. Joie had the perfect plan. "Tomorrow, you're going to get a new best friend at school."

Emily lifted her head. "How is that going to help me find a new mom?"

"I'm going to follow you around and see who is single and who likes you." Joie loved how quickly the idea popped into her head and smiled at her ingenuity.

"What about those?" Emily studied Joie's pointed ears. "They won't let you wear hats in school."

"Not to worry. I'll make sure no one sees them." Joie leaned forward and gave Emily a quick kiss on the forehead. Joie could hardly wait to get started on her assignment. This was going to be as easy as candy cane fudge. "I'll see you tomorrow."

CHAPTER SIX

Joie managed to hide her ears by securing them against her head with a little elf dust and then brushed her hair over them. The clothes she was wearing only needed slight modifications so that she looked like one of Emily's classmates and not an elf at all.

The hardest part had been slipping into the office and inputting her files into the school system. The easiest part was putting the note in the teacher's box. Mrs. Pritchard would accept her as a new student easily enough, as long as she didn't question administration.

Joie lined up alongside the other children.

Mrs. Pritchard went down the line of children and stopped at Joie. "Well, hello, little miss. You must be Joie."

"Yes, ma'am." Joie smiled brightly at the teacher. "We just moved to Miracle. My mom was going to wait until after Christmas to enroll me, but I just couldn't wait."

"We won't be doing much today, since it's the last day before the break."

Joie bounced on her toes. "I'm so excited for Christmas; are you?"

Mrs. Pritchard squatted beside Joie. "I love Christmas. It's my favorite time of year."

"Mine, too." Joie giggled.

"It must be with a last name like Noel." Mrs. Pritchard stood and faced the other children. "All right, you may follow me." She went to the front of the line and pushed Emily's wheelchair.

Joie moved along with the other children and entered a classroom almost as brightly decorated as the ones in North Pole Kingdom.

Mrs. Pritchard motioned to a desk. "You can sit here in the front of the room beside Emily Adams." It was the perfect size for Joie. She slipped into the seat, planted her feet on the floor and waited. She hadn't been in primary elf school for over fifteen years and tried to remember how to behave as a child.

After graduating from Elf University, Joie never thought she'd land back in the classroom, let alone in second grade, but Joie had a job to do. Surely, somewhere in this quaint little school, Joie could find a single woman who loved Emily.

The children had already filed in and took their seats. Mrs. Pritchard rolled Emily's wheelchair up to a desk, then leaned over and whispered to Joie. "You'll like Emily."

Mrs. Pritchard moved to the front of the classroom. "Class, we have a new student." She motioned to Joie. "This is Joie Noel. Their family just moved to town. Please be nice to her and say hello."

Emily smiled and leaned over. "Hi, Joie."

The boy sitting behind Emily poked the back of her head with his pencil. "She needs friends, not retards."

Joie turned to the blue eyed, blonde haired kid. "I'll bet you're on Santa's naughty list. Especially since you snooped and looked at all your presents."

Tommy's eyes widened. "I did not." Clearly, he was lying.

"And..." Joie drew the word out. "You got into your mom's phone and took pictures of your defecation in the toilet."

The boy narrowed his eyes. "What's defecation?"

Emily tilted her head to the side and smirked at Tommy. "Poop."

"Ew!" The girl sitting behind Tommy put her hand over her mouth.

"I did not." Tommy folded his arms with an emphatic huff.

Joie shrugged. "Well, that's not what your elf told me."

"All right children, quiet down now." Mrs. Pritchard motioned for Tommy to stop talking.

Tommy stuck out his tongue at Joie. The girl behind him, Lyssa, if Joie remembered right, rolled her eyes at him and turned toward the teacher.

Joie had loved elf elementary school when she was a kid, especially foreign languages. It gave her lots of opportunities to visit children all over the world. She leaned close to Emily and whispered. "What about her? She's young, pretty, and I can tell she loves kids. Of course, you have to love children to be a teacher."

"She's already married."

"Oh." Joie pulled her mouth into a pout. She'd never been good with human adult situations. Elves stopped reporting naughty and nice lists once children quit believing in Santa. If only they still believed, they might just not do some of the rotten things they did, thinking there was an elf watching them. Even the idea of heaven recording all of their doings didn't seem to deter some adults from making bad choices.

At recess, Joie pushed Emily down the hall. "Who are some of the other adults that you might consider?"

Emily pointed to each of the doors as they passed other classrooms. "Miss Hall is really nice."

Joie stood on her tip toes and looked through the window. The red headed woman with a rosy complexion was pretty. Her body had nice, round curves. "Does your dad like them plump?"

Emily giggled. "You mean fat?"

"She's not fat. Miss Hall has all the right curves." Joie thought about Mrs. Claus. She was just right. But then Santa was portly so he probably didn't mind that his wife was just right, like Miss Hall.

"Maybe." Emily sounded doubtful.

Joie ducked down when Miss Hall looked her way. "I think we should get her to meet your dad."

"How are we going to do that? She doesn't even teach my same grade. She's fifth. We're only second."

Joie smiled. "We'll have to think of a way to get your dad to come here to pick you up." Joie snapped her fingers. "I have it."

"What?" Emily asked as Joie continued to roll her down the hall.

"You pretend to get sick right at the end of school. Your dad will have to come get you." Joie's brain was going faster than the Candy Cane Express around a Christmas tree. "And then, just watch as I make some magic happen."

CHAPTER SEVEN

Matt raced into the school building and straight to the nurse's office. Emily leaned on her arm rest, her chin against her knuckles.

"Hi, Daddy." She looked up at him, her mouth drooping.

His gut tightened. He hated when she got sick. It usually meant a trip to urgent care several towns over, or the emergency room in the next county if it was late at night. "What's wrong, cupcake?"

"My tummy hurts." She rubbed her belly. "I think I'm going to throw up." Emily grabbed the bowl the nurse had put in her lap, although nothing came up.

He sucked a deep breath and held in his own nausea. "Let's get you home."

The nurse came into the room. "I have a release I need for you to sign."

Matt scribbled his name and phone number onto it after he'd read the *Sick Child* report.

"Thank you, Mr. Adams for coming so quickly." She bent so that her face was level with Emily's. "I hope you feel better soon. This is a crummy way to start your Christmas break."

"Thank you, Ms. Evans." Emily smiled weakly at the nurse.

Taking the curved bowl from Emily, Matt held it out to Ms. Evans.

She didn't take it. "Keep it. You might need it later."

"Thank you." This wasn't the first time Matt had to get his daughter from school. It *was* the first time he'd actually taken the time to look at Ms. Evans. Her blond hair and brown eyes contrasted sharply with her dark skin. Quite a beautiful woman, but not like his Cadence. It had been two whole years since his wife's death. Craig had urged him to start looking, had tried to set him up a couple of times. Disasters, all of them. Maybe it was time for him to look on his own, without outside help.

He tried to think of a way to find out if she might be single. His stomach tightened.

Ms. Evans broke the awkward silence. "I'm sure it's just a touch of a stomach bug. She'll probably be fine tomorrow."

"Are you married?" Why had he said that? What an idiot. He should have been a little more subtle.

Ms. Evans's head shot up from where she'd been looking over Matt's signature. "Excuse me?"

"I'm sorry. That was totally inappropriate." Why had his brain turned to mush? Matt gripped the handles on Emily's chair and wheeled her out the door before he could make a bigger mess of things.

Once they were out of earshot of the front office, Emily leaned her head back. "If you must know, Ms. Evans is single, but I think she's dating someone."

"And how would you know this?" Matt couldn't believe a child would know so much about the affairs of the nurse.

"Because she was on the phone one time when I was in her office and she was talking all sweet to someone."

"Oh." Matt couldn't think of anything else to say.

The bell rang, releasing students in a steady stream out various doors carrying bags of goodies, pictures, and papers. Since it was the last day before Christmas break, parents who normally let their children ride home, or take the bus had congested the parking lot, blocking Matt's truck. He'd hoped to grab Emily and leave before the after-school mob hemmed him in. "Well, sugar, it looks like we might be here a bit. Do you mind?"

"No. I think I'll be okay." Emily handed him the bowl.

"You better keep it just in case." He tossed it on the backseat of his truck before turning to Emily. He lifted her into the back passenger seat and buckled her in and then stowed her wheelchair into the bed.

After he got in and buckled himself, Emily wailed from the back seat. "Daddy, I forgot my backpack. It's in my classroom."

Matt leaned back on the headrest. He'd left a huge contract they'd been trying to finish on account the unseasonably heavy rain, and now he was going to be late getting back. "Oh, Em, can't you just get it after Christmas?"

"My art project is in it. I want to work on it."

"All right." He got out of the truck and tucked his keys into his pocket. "I'll lock the door and you sit right there. Don't talk to anyone. I'll be right back."

Matt bounded up the stairs and fought the stream of kids exiting. He reached Emily's classroom and hurried through the door. "Emily forgot her backpack."

Mrs. Prichard looked up from a stack of papers. "Oh, Mr. Adams, I sent it with her to the nurse's office."

Another delay? "Thank you." He bit back frustration.

"I hope she feels better."

"Me, too." He didn't want to mention that time was money and he was losing plenty by Emily's illness. Yet, he'd do anything for his Em. She was all he had left. He also did not want another encounter with the nurse. Suck it up, cowboy.

Matt knocked on the nurse's door.

A complete lack of surprise covered her face as she held out Emily's backpack. "Forget something?" It dangled from her finger as if she might be afraid to come in contact with Matt.

"Thank you." He reached for the bag and she snatched it back.

"I'm not married." Her face did not blush as she said it. "And as a thank you for holding her pack for her, you may treat me to a cup of hot cocoa. Meet me at SweetHart's Cafe at seven o'clock tonight."

Matt felt like a buffalo waiting for the slaughter. "Sure?"

She held Emily's backpack out to him again. "Wonderful. Olivia whips up the best peppermint hot chocolate this side of Houston."

CHAPTER
EIGHT

Joie sat next to Emily in the back seat. "You did great!"

"I'm getting pretty good at pretending to be sick. It sure gets me out of a lot of school." Emily smiled and tossed the barf tray onto the floor. "You should have seen me pretend to gag. Even my dad looked like he was going to be sick, too."

"And look." Joie pointed to Miss Hall exiting the building, heading to her car.

Emily giggled. "Did you really let the air out of her tire?"

"See for yourself." She nodded at the fifth-grade teacher.

Miss Hall got into her car and backed it out a couple of feet, then put it into park. She climbed out and eyed the driver's side front tire. Yep, flat as a gumdrop run over by a reindeer.

"And nobody saw you?" Emily asked.

"Not a soul. I'm magical that way." Joie glanced up in time to see Matthew coming down the front sidewalk toward the truck.

Most of the parents had cleared the road which meant Matt would probably want to hurry away. Joie couldn't let that happen. "Tell your dad about Miss Hall." Joie winked out, but continued to monitor the situation.

Matt unlocked the door and slid into the seat, jamming his key into the ignition.

"Daddy, look." Emily pointed to Miss Hall. "Her tire's flat. You should go help her."

For the second time, Matt leaned his head back. "Sweetheart, I'm sure there are lots of other people around who can help her. She can call her husband even."

"She doesn't have a husband and all the other parents are gone." Emily's voice sounded pleading and concerned.

Joie stifled a snicker so she wouldn't give herself away. Emily was doing a fine job.

With a frustrated sigh, Matt pulled the key from the ignition and walked over to Miss Hall. Invisible, Joie followed close behind careful not to bump into them.

"Looks like you have a flat tire." Matt rubbed the back of his head, ruffling his brown hair.

Joie rolled her eyes. No kidding, Gumdrop.

"Thank you, Captain Obvious." Miss Hall had already gone to the back of her car and popped the trunk.

"Can I give you a hand with that?" Matt tried to take the tire from her.

"Nope. My daddy taught me how to do all kinds of things for myself." She let the tire fall to the ground.

Joie pinched her lips. Who knew Miss Hall could be so self-sufficient. She'd just have to help things along a little bit.

Joie gave a flick of her fingers and the tire rolled down the sloping drive. Both Matt and Miss Hall chased after it. Crossing the street, it glided without mishap and landed on a grassy field on the other side.

Matt screeched to a halt as Miss Hall slammed into the back of him, obviously not expecting him to stop like that. The momentum propelled him into the street, and he narrowly missed getting hit by a truck.

Spinning around he stepped back to the side of the road and grabbed her by her shoulders. "You stay here."

Joie had not expected for Miss Hall to push him like that. It almost got him killed.

Miss Hall stepped around him. "It's my tire." She waited until the cars had passed and crossed the street.

Matt looked at her as if he couldn't decide if he should follow her just to make sure she got back across the street or leave her to fend for herself. With another frustrated sigh, he crossed the road. "Seriously, ma'am, let me help you with that."

Miss Hall had started to roll it back the way they'd come. She looked down at her now dirty hands, the black streak on her cream skirt, and then back at Matt. "Fine."

Joie didn't think that sounded like a *fine* fine, but rather an "if-you-must fine." Miss Hall did not look happy about it at all.

Matt managed to get the tire back across the street and replaced with the flat one. Once Miss Hall was on her way, Joie frowned. That teacher didn't even say thank you.

"That is not what I expected," Joie said out loud.

Matt snapped around, backing up. "Who said that?" His foot caught the edge of the curb and he went down with a hard thunk on the pavement.

Joie slapped her hand over her mouth. She had to stop frightening the poor guy or she'd never get Emily her Christmas wish.

CHAPTER NINE

Matt rubbed his backside and looked around, hoping no one had seen him make a fool of himself. He was sure he'd heard that voice again. Ms. Evans stood at the window and gave him a little wave. Of all the people to see him fall...

Once he got into the truck, he turned to Emily. A frown had settled on her usually bright face. "You okay, pumpkin?"

"I thought you'd want to ask Miss Hall out on a date."

Matt tried to keep his chuckle inside. "I don't even know Miss Hall, and she certainly didn't give me any chance to introduce myself, let alone ask her out."

Emily's face brightened. "I know. You could send her a Christmas card telling her your name and that you were the one who helped her with her tire. Then you write down your phone number. She'll probably call you and ask *you* out on a date as a thank you. We can deliver it to her tomorrow since the teachers have to be here to do grading and stuff. That way you don't have to mail it."

This time Matt didn't try to hide his laughter. "That woman was about as friendly as a porcupine." He eyed her in the rear-view mirror. “Leave the match-making to me, okay?” He put his key in the ignition and started the truck.

A long sigh escaped Emily. “O...kay....” She wiggled against her seatbelt. “Joie said it would work.”

Matt spun around. “What do you mean – Joie?”

“She’s an elf all the way from the north pole.” Glee filled Emily’s voice.

“Joie is not an elf. She’s a prank set up by either Craig or one of the other guys.” Matt put his truck in reverse. “And I don’t think Miss Hall is in on the prank.” Neither was that nurse, Ms. Evans. He shook his head thinking about how foolish he’d acted in her office and then again on the sidewalk. Had she been watching him the whole time trying to help Miss Hall? If the faculty had some kind of Christmas send-off tomorrow, they’d certainly have something to gossip about.

It didn’t help that Ms. Evans had asked him to meet her at Sweet-Hart’s Cafe. Demanded, actually. Maybe he could transfer Emily to another school.

“Joie’s just trying to help.” Emily played with her backpack strap, a pout forming on her lip.

Matt glanced at Emily as he navigated the road. “For someone who’s supposed to be sick, you’re pretty chipper all of a sudden.”

“That’s because Joie told me to pretend to be sick. That way you could meet Miss Hall and ask her on a date.” Her eyes looked so hopeful.

“Look, young lady, you shouldn’t be doing things like that. I have a company to run and you need to be in school learning, and you tell Joie the next time you see her that I will find my own dates.” *Thank you very much, Craig for being so awful.*

The man could never let a good joke on Matt go unpunished. This time he’d taken it to the extreme. If Craig wasn’t his partner, he’d fire him.

“You can tell Joie yourself. She’s right here.” Emily pointed at the seat beside her.

“Hi, Matthew.” Joie waved at him.

Matt slammed on the breaks and swerved off the road, narrowly missing a light pole. His heart racing, he put the truck in park and turned around to see Joie sitting beside Emily. He got out of his truck and opened the back door. "How do you keep getting into my truck?"

"I told you, I'm an elf."

Joie's cute smile was not going to get to him this time. He stuck his finger in her face. "Young lady, where is your mother?"

"Dad, wait!" Emily practically shouted. "She really is an elf."

Joie pulled her hair back, exposing pointed ears.

Matt took a deep breath. There was no such thing as Santa. So why was he having an argument with a girl who looked like an elf? Those ears had to be fake. Right now was not the time to debate about the validity of Santa Claus when his daughter still believed. "All right, Joie. Since you obviously missed your bus, I suppose I should take you home. Where do you live?"

"219 Sugar Plum Lane, Elf District, North Pole." Joie chuckled. "But I don't think you can drive me there."

This little mischief maker had certainly learned her part well.

"I am the real deal." Joie smiled back at him. "Look, I know that we got off to a bad start last night, but I'd like to show you that I only mean to help you find a wife."

Matt frowned, furrowing his brows. This whole thing was getting out of hand. "Elf or not, you can't ride in my truck without being buckled in." He pulled the strap across her securing her the best he could without a booster seat.

Emily clapped her hands. "Then she can come home and play?"

"Only if I can get hold of her parents." Then pulling his cell phone out, he asked. "What's your parent's phone number?"

"907-N-R-T-H-P-O-L, or in numeric it's 907-678-7653."

Matt punched in the number. Surprised when *Here Comes Santa Claus* played, he waited for an answer. "North Pole Kingdom," the young male voice on the other end said.

Pulling the phone away from his ear, he checked the number he'd just dialed. That couldn't be Alaska, could it? "I'd like to speak with the parents of a little girl named Joie."

"Oh, hold one moment." The music came back on.

"Did you live in Alaska before you moved here?" Matt asked, eying Joie where she sat with a grin spread across her face.

The music stopped. "This is Laila."

"Hello Laila, this is Matthew Adams. I have your little one with me and she wanted to come home with Emily." Matt continued to eye Joie.

"Oh, I'm so glad she's with you." Laila's voice didn't sound the least bit concerned, but more amused.

"What time would you like me to bring her home?" Matt asked.

"No need. She knows the way." Laila chuckled and then hung up.

Matt shook his head. Some parents really needed to learn how to be more concerned about their children. There was no way he was going to let a child walk home alone. Maybe he should report them to Child Protective Services.

"Joie can stay for an hour and then I have to get ready for a not-date with Ms. Evans." Matt returned to the driver's seat. "We need to make a stop by the site, make sure things are going well with the Winston's home."

"My daddy builds houses and stuff." The pride shone through Emily's voice.

"Me, too!" Joie practically bubbled with excitement. "Maybe I can help."

Matt shook his head. This was one seriously delusional child. Maybe Laila needed a break from her antics.

The whole drive across town, Matt had to listen to a barrage of questions from Emily. "How many elves live at the north pole?"

"Last count, I think there's two-thousand, six hundred and forty-four. That's accounting for the sixty-two births this year and four deaths."

Matt followed Peach Drive alongside the pastures, glancing in the rearview mirror from time to time.

"What's Santa's favorite cookie?" Emily asked.

"Gingerbread!" From the sound of Joie's voice, it was hers as well.

Emily clapped her hands and pointed at Matt. "See Dad, I told you it wasn't sugar cookies."

"Fine, we'll buy gingerbread this year." Matt shook his head and kept his eyes on the road.

"Sorry, Mr. Adams, but Santa likes them fresh baked." The closer Matt looked at Joie, the less she looked like a child. Something about her seemed mature. Joie continued, "But it's okay to keep doing sugar cookies. He likes those, too. Anyway, everyone at the North Pole knows you couldn't make a decent cookie if you tried."

Matt's grip on the steering wheel tightened. Of course, he couldn't make cookies. He could barely put a microwave dinner on the table. The cooking and baking department had been Cadence's.

"How does Santa get to all the children all over the world in just one night?" Emily asked.

The answer to that one was a no brainer. Matt adjusted the rear view mirror so he could see both of the girls. "Time stands still while he makes his deliveries. He also gets lots of parents to help."

Joie put her hand to her chin and raised her eyebrows. "Actually, that's a fallacy perpetrated by Einstein. Which is, the faster Santa's reindeer fly, the closer he approaches the speed of light." Joie chuckled. "Really, can you just imagine the sleigh catching fire at that speed?"

"All right then, what's your theory?" He hoped she didn't tell the truth. It would ruin Christmas for Emily.

"Santa Claus is a master wizard, and he winks his sleigh and reindeer from house to house." Her expression looked far too confident.

"Then why does he even need reindeer at all?" He'd caught her. "I mean since he can just wink himself into every child's house."

"You're right, he could do that." She shrugged and chuckled. "But what fun would Christmas be if at least one or two children didn't hear reindeer paws on the rooftops?"

Matt rolled his eyes. That was the dumbest explanation ever. "All right, I have another question for you."

"Sure."

"How is it that Santa's wrapping paper is the same as the parents of the children he delivers to? I'll bet Santa drops off the paper, and parents just wrapped up the gifts for their kids from the left overs." Matt had her there.

"Actually, Santa always has elves that are watching and they go back and report to Santa which ones the parents use and he uses the same kind."

Matt shook his head. Did Joie have to contradict everything he said?

"And the cookies and milk? How can one man eat that much in one night and not get sick?"

Emily raised her hand. "Oh, I know!"

Matt went from watching the road to the girls in the back seat. "You do, huh?"

Emily smiled and nodded. "Mrs. Claus gives Santa a special drink before he leaves; one that makes the cookies and milk disappear in his tummy."

"That's right!" Joie patted Emily's hand. "You're a very smart girl."

"By the way," Joie interrupted his thoughts. "I'll be monitoring your date tonight to make sure things go well. Since the flat tire didn't work out with Miss Hall, I'll take extra care not to mess this one up."

Matt's head snapped up. "How did you know about Ms. Evans?"

"I told you. I'm an elf. Kids aren't the only ones that elves spy on."

CHAPTER
TEN

Once they reached the Winston house, Joie eyed the unfinished Victorian home. The blue-gray siding completed the first story. A man stood on a scaffolding shooting nails into the wooden panels on the second floor. This was almost the same as the first dollhouse she'd helped build. From the top of the parapet and balconies down to the wide, wrap-around porches, this home spoke of wealth. She could just imagine what it would look like when it was finished; pine garlands with fairy lights wrapping the columns, a Christmas tree in the big picture window, and the aroma of gingerbread filling the corners of the house, beckoning the children into the kitchen.

Joie sighed with the memories of home. Mrs. Claus's kitchen never sat empty of delectable treats. She desperately wanted to see the inside of the Winston home; it might give her ideas for her next dollhouse.

Matt got out of the car. "Now, you girls don't go in the house. There are too many things for you to get hurt on." He pointed to a scrap wood pile beside the front door. "Maybe you can take the pieces and stack them like blocks. Just watch your fingers for splinters."

He grabbed an old quilt from the floor behind the seat and carried Emily to the front porch. After he spread out the quilt, he set her on the ground beside the pile of wood. "I'll be back in a bit."

"How come he didn't put you in your wheelchair?" Joie asked, sitting beside her on the blanket.

Emily shifted and pushed her legs straight out. "He does that sometimes. I guess it's easier than getting out my wheelchair every time."

Joie nodded. "He's a really nice guy, isn't he?"

Emily smiled. "He's super nice."

"Hmm..." Joie glanced through the window. Matt ascended the sweeping staircase and disappeared out of sight. "He doesn't believe I'm an elf." She'd tried several times to convince him. What more did she need to do?

"I believe you."

Joie gathered a few pieces of cut lumber. "I know you do. And I suppose it doesn't matter if I can't convince him. I can still get the job done."

Emily fell over trying to reach a couple of the pieces before righting herself. She stacked them in front of her. "I guess so."

Joie would rather have gone inside to check out the building instead of playing with Emily, not that she didn't enjoy the child. Emily's determination and bright spirit were contagious. It made Joie want to try all the harder to find a perfect match for Matt.

A high-pitched squeal at the far end of the porch brought Joie around to face a wild boar. Its head swung from side to side, pointed tusks protruding from the side of its mouth. With a low grunt, it bounded toward Emily.

Fear prickled Joie's scalp. She couldn't let the nasty creature attack them. She jumped to her feet and screamed, "Matt!" praying he'd heard her.

The animal charged, leaving no time for Matt to reach them before the enraged animal attacked. In a split second, Joie knew what she had to do. She sprinted toward the red-eyed hog.

Advancing on them, the boar swept past Joie and headed straight toward Emily. Screaming, she tried to scramble away using her arms, her legs dragging behind her.

"Hey!" Joie screamed at the boar and sprinted across the porch. Once she grabbed its tail, it squealed again and turned toward Joie, yanking the tail from her hands. Surprised, it backed up, then lowered its head, preparing to ram her. It lunged, and before Joie could move out of the way, it knocked her off her feet, and sent her sailing over its back. She landed hard on the wood planks. It turned and bore down on her, its snout ramming her hip, rolling her over and over. Finally able to grab ahold of one of its front legs she thrust her feet under its belly, and with her inner strength and agility, she flipped it off the porch. It landed in the mud below. At least now it couldn't reach them. It shook itself off and charged the pilon holding up the porch. Before she gave it a thought, Joie gripped the charm on her bracelet and in a flash of light aimed it at the beast. The boar dropped to the ground rolled to one side and vanished, leaving a layer of gray dust that dissipated into the soggy ground.

Matt ran to her side and knelt beside her. "What were you thinking, tackling a wild hog? Are you all right?"

Joie slumped back onto the wood and breathed heavily. "Just a little bruised, I think." Polar bears had a nicer disposition; she'd rather tackle one of those any day. With a groan, she stood and checked her ribs. It didn't feel like anything was broken and her bracelet was intact. At least she still had four of the miracles left. Hopefully, she wouldn't need to use the rest of them on experiences like this.

Behind them, Emily sobbed. "Daddy, Daddy."

Matt sprinted back to his daughter, slunk down next to her, and gathered her onto his lap. "Oh, baby, I'm so sorry."

Emily buried her head in his chest and continued to cry.

Joie sat beside them both and patted Emily's shoulder. "That was scary, huh?"

"I don't know where that boar came from. I haven't seen any

around here lately. They usually stay in the woods." Matt's eyes widened. "You saved Emily's life."

Joie shrugged. "I guess that's part of my mission here, too. It would be rather pointless to find a mother for Emily if she'd died."

Matt slowly nodded his head. "What happened to the boar?"

Joie pushed a lock of hair off her forehead. "He's gone – permanently. I had to use a miracle on him."

CHAPTER
ELEVEN

After making dinner for Emily and Joie, Matt went into his bedroom to get ready to meet Ms. Evans. He swallowed, and tightened his grip on the collar of his shirt as he fought to make it lay straight. How did that little bit of a thing manage to wrestle a boar? It had to have been three or four-hundred pounds. It should have killed her or at the very least landed her in the hospital. Yet, she didn't seem to have a scratch on her. As for the boar, it had disappeared. The only evidence it had ever existed was an impression of its body where it had lain in the mud.

If he admitted the child was really an elf, someone might have him committed. Insanity did not run in his family.

Emily called from downstairs, "Dad. I'm done."

Matt went to the kitchen, dumped her empty paper plate and plastic fork in the trash.

Joie nibbled at the food on her plate. "You could use a few cooking lessons. I'm sure Mrs. Claus has some recipes that might be easy enough for you."

"Thank you." Matt glared at her. "I'll ask for her cookbook for Christmas."

Before Joie could respond, Emily tugged on his pant leg and smiled up at him. "You sure look handsome for your date."

He pointed to Joie's plate. "When you're done eating you can join us." He picked Emily up out of her wheelchair and took her upstairs with him. "How many times do I have to tell you, it's not a date?"

"Joie says that anytime you meet a woman who wants to eat or drink with you, it's a date." Her face lit with excitement. "And I really like Ms. Evans. She's always nice to me."

Matt set her on the bed and went back to the mirror over his dresser. After fighting with the collar again, he gave up on the wrinkled shirt. Cadence would have ironed it flat. But then, if his wife was still alive, he wouldn't have agreed to meet Ms. Evans for hot chocolate.

Matt unbuttoned his shirt and tossed it in the closet. "Well, your little elf friend has interfered enough."

"Joie also says that you need to go on at least ten dates before you can decide if she's the right one for you." Emily smiled up at him. "But, Dad, you're getting older and so am I. I need a mother. So if you want to propose to Ms. Evans tonight that would be okay."

Matt's gut tightened in dread at the thought of dating. "This is not a date. I promise I shall not be proposing to her tonight." He paused. "Or ever."

"Then why are you going out with her?"

"Because, well..." Matt had already asked himself that same question several times and hadn't come up with his own plausible answer.

"Because he's trying on shoes." Joie said where she sat on the bed next to Emily.

Matt jumped and swore. When had she come in?

"That's a bad word, Daddy." Emily frowned at him. "You should have your mouth washed out."

He ignored his daughter and turned his attention on...the elf. There, he'd admitted it. "Do you have to keep popping in and out like that?"

"I'm sorry, next time I'll knock." Joie scooted to the edge of the bed. "Dating is like trying on shoes. Some shoes are too tight, some are too wide, and some fit just right."

"Oh, like Cinderella. Kind of. But instead of finding the princess who fits the shoe, Daddy has to find the shoe to fit the prince."

"That's right." Joie looked up at Matt. "And your father is one prince of a guy."

Matt put his hands on his hips. "All right you two, stop talking about me as if I wasn't here."

Emily looked up at him with hopeful eyes. "Are you going to be nice to her?"

"I am being nice to her." He smirked at the elf – he had been convinced after the boar incident. There was no way a child could take on a beast that size. "I suppose I'd better or she'll tell Santa I've been naughty, and he won't bring me any presents."

"I meant Ms. Evans, Dad. Sheesh." Emily rolled her eyes.

"I'm not going to get married just because you need a mother." Matt didn't even know why he'd agreed to meet Ms. Evans in the first place.

Tears welled up in Emily's eyes and trailed down her cheeks.

"Oh, Em." Matt's heart melted at the sight of his precious daughter. He hadn't thought about her emotional needs since Cadence died. He'd been so busy making sure to take her to doctor's appointments, keeping her fed and clothed, that he'd forgotten she had a broken heart as well. Her love for her mother must have left a hole in her so big that Matt had walked right through it, never touching the edges.

He knelt down and placed a hand under her chin. "Of course, I'll be nice to her."

"I'll make sure they even share a goodnight kiss." Joie touched Matt's shoulder.

Shrugging her hand off, he turned to Joie. "And don't follow me. I can handle this on my own."

Matt pulled a light blue shirt from the closet. As he buttoned it up, his cell phone rang – his babysitter.

"Hey Mr. Adams, I am so sorry to have to cancel on you tonight. My mom forgot she had a church thing, and I have to stay and watch my little brother and sister."

"All right, perhaps another night." He clicked the end button and set the phone on his dresser. Maybe he wasn't supposed to go out with Ms. Evans after all. It wasn't like they had an actual date. Then again, how would that look standing her up? And he would have to face her at some future date when he picked up Emily again. He wished he'd thought to get her phone number before he left the nurse's office.

"Maybe Grandma can watch you two." He hated the idea of his mother finding out he was going to meet a woman for a drink. She'd be sending out wedding invitations before the evening was even through.

When he tried calling her, the phone went straight to voicemail. It was just like her to let it go dead and forget to charge it.

"All right, the two of you are just going to have to come with me." Matt scooped up his jacket and tossed it over his arm.

"You'll never kiss her if I go," Emily whined when he tucked her in his other arm.

"I'd never kiss her on a first date, and this is not a date." Taking the girls along with him was the perfect solution. He'd made sure that he didn't stay too long.

Joie slid off the bed. "I can babysit for you."

"Just because you can boar wrestle doesn't mean that you..."

Joie rolled her eyes. "I'm twenty-six. I've had my share of caring for children. We do have them at the North Pole, you know. And it just so happens that I like to wrestle polar bears for fun. I'm confident I can take care of an eight year old child."

"In a wheelchair. What if something happens and you have to lift her?"

Joie raised her eyebrows, mocking him, then motioned for him to hand Emily to her. "Let me show you." She held out her arms.

Matt kept Emily's weight supported.

Snatching Emily from Matt, Joie turned and left the bedroom. He followed behind them and his heart missed a beat when she carried Emily down the stairs.

Matt raced after them, preparing to catch them if Joie stumbled.

"See? Easy as cinnamon apple crunch cake." Joie set Emily in her wheelchair.

Elf or not, she still looked about the same age as his daughter. "You're twenty-six?"

Joie put her hand up her sleeve and pulled out a card and handed it to him. "Proof."

Joie Noel, Born December 25, 1992

Employment: Wonderful Woodworking

Employee of the month April, June, July, August, September, October, November 2018

He eyed her photo and the information below. "What happened to May?"

Joie crossed her arms. "I was out sick with peppermint fever and lost my perfect attendance."

Matt handed the card back to Joie. "Let me try calling Grandma one more time." After it went to voicemail, he sent a text. "I'm meeting someone for hot chocolate, can you check in on Emily?" Then deleted it. His mother would be furious when she found out he'd left two girls alone together, never mind that Joie was an extraordinary elf. He hadn't even believed it himself until today.

"Please, Daddy?" Emily sent Matt that look, the one he could never resist.

He ran his hand over his face. SweetHart's Cafe was only a few miles away and he could be back in an instant if anything went wrong. Matt couldn't believe he was even considering it. "No, you're both coming with me."

Emily slammed her fist down on the armrest. "You'll never kiss her if we're there."

"I'm not going to kiss her." He stood considering his options. He shouldn't. He really shouldn't, as in really-really shouldn't. "All right. I'll lock the doors. I'll be back in thirty minutes." He shook his finger at both of them. "Don't do anything other than watch a movie."

"Yes!" Emily held out her hand for a high five with Joie.

He couldn't believe he'd agreed to such a hair-brained notion. Did Joie cast some kind of spell over him? Matt took a deep breath. "I'll be back in thirty minutes."

CHAPTER TWELVE

As soon as Matt walked out the door, Joie shut off the television. She'd seen that Christmas movie a hundred times, had even been sent on special assignment to make sure the producers represented the elves correctly. It seemed that every time elves showed up in films, they were childish and simple minded, especially that horrible one streaming this year. *Terrible* and *horrible* hardly touched how they'd ruined the movie.

Joie looked around the living room. "Why don't you have a Christmas tree?"

Emily shrugged. "I don't know. We didn't have one last year, either."

The living room could have held one in every corner for how spacious it was with its vaulted ceilings and a balcony over the far end of the living room where the bedrooms were. "That is something I intend to remedy right away."

"A real tree." Emily's eyes lit up. "As tall as the roof, except maybe not quite that high, because we need to put the star on top."

"And lots of red and gold ornaments, and we have to string popcorn and cranberries." Joie loved decorating the trees in North

Pole Kingdom. Mrs. Claus told her that if she did her job well she'd get to head the Bright Twinkle department. She had lots of ideas to make the place sparkle.

Emily clapped her hands. "As soon as Daddy gets home from his not-date, you can talk him into getting one."

"Yes," Joie said, excited at the prospects of incorporating some of her concepts. "We can run garland up the hand rails with twinkling lights." She practically floated around the room. "I can sew some red plaid chair covers and matching pillows for the sofa."

"Can we put a train around the tree?" Emily bounced in her wheelchair.

Joie turned to Emily. "Of course. What is Christmas without one chug-chugging along its track?" Spying the fireplace, Joie put her hands on her hips and shook her head. "This will never do."

"What?"

"Do you have a stocking?" She crossed to the mantle and ran her finger over the dust. "We'll need to whip this house into shape."

A soft giggle escaped Emily. "This will be the best Christmas ever."

She turned to Emily. "Now then, how about we make some gingerbread cookies?"

Emily pulled the corners of her mouth into a frown and then her face lit up. "I love gingerbread cookies."

"Excellent. Before we start in on the house, we need to make it smell like Christmas in here, don't you think?" Joie didn't wait for Emily to answer, but went straight to the kitchen.

Emily wheeled her chair to the doorway. Her face had brightened. "I can tell you where everything is."

"Your father is going to be so impressed." Joie smiled at Emily. The child needed a mother to bake cookies with, to decorate the house and to do things that mothers and daughters did together. Hopefully, Ms. Evans would work out after all. She was an awfully smart woman, and she loved kids, especially ones who needed extra attention.

Emily pointed as she spoke. "The bowls are in that cupboard, and all the baking stuff is in that one."

Joie took a mixing bowl and set it on the table in front of Emily. "Your mother sure liked her kitchen organized, huh? And it's still organized."

"That's because Daddy never bakes anything. But Mommy used to make the best cookies," Emily said with a sigh.

Joie set the oven temperature and went to the refrigerator for butter and eggs. "And we're going to make some just like your mother used to make."

CHAPTER THIRTEEN

Matt checked his hair in the visor mirror once more, then gripped the steering wheel. What had he gotten himself into? He checked his phone and made sure the timer still counted down. Thirty minutes until it vibrated in his pocket, signaling enough time to get her phone number – in case he wanted a real date with her – and get out of the cafe before he committed to anything but a drink.

With a quick exhalation he stepped out of his truck and into the frosty air, cold enough for snow. The stars shined brightly overhead as he thought of his wife. "Well, Cadence, I hope you don't mind."

"It's Clara." Ms. Evans linked her arm in his. "It seems we got here at the same time."

"Clara." Startled, he nodded and led her up the walkway to the only hotel with the only restaurant in town. "Am I allowed to call you that?"

She laughed and the sound of it surprised Matt. Delightful, like sunshine in the spring. "Why wouldn't you call me by my first name? What do you usually call me?"

Matt opened the door for Ms. Evans. "I don't know...the nurse."

"I'm only that by day." She chuckled again and dropped her hand as the hostess met them. "Two please."

"This way." The hostess led them through the nearly empty room to a booth in the back and set two glasses of water and their menus in front of them.

Matt motioned for her to sit. He took the other side so he could watch the door. "I can't stay long...you know how elves like to hurry back to the North Pole." Matt tried to make it sound like a joke, except if he told her the truth she might get up and walk out the door. Tempting. However, he didn't want his sanity questioned.

Clara picked up the paper menu and perused it. "What do elves have to do with anything?"

Matt let out a nervous chuckle. "I have one babysitting my Emily."

She set the menu down. "That's funny. I never knew you had such a clever sense of humor."

Chewing the inside of his cheek, he picked up his menu. He didn't dare tell her the elf on the shelf – or at least the one on the couch – was real and that she was babysitting his daughter. He wondered what CPS would do if they found two children at home alone. Nobody was going to buy that Joie was an elf. He swallowed.

"You seem awful nervous. You're not scared of me, are you?" She reached across the table and put her hand on his.

Yes, he was, but Matt wasn't about to admit it out loud. Without looking like he didn't welcome her touch, he pulled his hand away and reached for his glass of water, taking a long drink so as not to answer her.

"I'm starving," Clara said when Matt didn't answer. "I think I'll have an appetizer to start off the meal."

Matt swallowed again. He didn't want to be gone that long. He'd promised Joie he'd be back in a half hour. It would take fifteen minutes after they ordered, and then how long to eat? What kind of emergency could he come up with to pull himself away?

A waitress crossed the room, stopping at their table. "What can I get y'all?"

Clara ran a finger over her menu. "The fried platter."

"Excellent." She scribbled on her pad. "The zucchinis are hot-house grown this time of year."

Matt coughed. "I'll take a hot chocolate."

Clara put her menu down. "Oh, he'll have more than that. How about a thick, juicy steak? Sirloin?"

The waitress turned to Matt. "How would you like that cooked?"

Matt glared at Clara, but she wasn't paying any attention to him as she'd gone back to perusing the menu. "Can you give me a minute? I'm not sure what I want," she said.

"Yes, please, give us a moment." Matt rolled his eyes and pushed his menu away.

"I'll get your appetizer going and be back in a minute." The waitress strode to the kitchen.

Matt picked up his menu, trying to find something quick to fix and quicker to eat. Not steak – that would take forever. So much for hot chocolate only. He set his menu back down. "Look, Clara, I only meant to meet you for a drink. I told my sitter I'd be gone for a half hour."

Clara blinked her eyes as if not comprehending what he said. "Oh, I thought we could have a nice meal and then – "

Matt cut her off. "There is no *and then.* We agreed on a cup of hot chocolate. You can go ahead and order what you want."

Her lip turned down in a pout. "It's no fun to eat all alone."

"Fine, we'll eat the appetizer *and then* I have to go." Matt grimaced. Ms. Evans was definitely not the woman for him. He needed someone who would let him take the lead. Not that he was chauvinistic, he just didn't like being railroaded.

Within a few minutes, the waitress returned with a platter of fried zucchini, mozzarella sticks, and onion rings.

She shuffled pieces onto her plate and took the entire cup of dipping sauce. Matt had no idea how she managed to stay thin eating as she did. "Sho Mahht..." With her mouth stuffed full, he could hardly understand her. "Do you have any plans for Christmas?"

Before he could answer, the waitress came to the table. "Now then about your order."

Clara smiled. "I'll have the sirloin steak, medium. And Matt here will have the same."

"Don't forget the hot cocoa," Matt said in defeat.

CHAPTER
FOURTEEN

The timer dinged, and Joie pulled a perfect batch of ginger cookies shaped like little men out of the oven. "They smell almost like Mrs. Claus's kitchen." Contented with her accomplishment, she took the spatula and lifted them onto the cookie rack and set them on the table to cool.

Emily rolled her chair to the kitchen table. "I'll bet they taste like it, too." She reached for one.

Joie waggled her finger. "Uh, uh, uh. Not until they're ready to frost.

A sizzle and pop sent Joie spinning back to the stove, at the same time the smoke detector blared its warning. Several papers sitting near the stove flamed up to the ceiling, spreading orange and yellow fingers across the kitchen.

Joie screamed.

"What?" Emily craned her neck around. She matched Joie's high pitched scream. "Fire! Fire!"

Joie grabbed Emily's wheelchair and rushed her out the front door. "Do you have a cell phone?"

Emily shook her head.

"Fire extinguisher?"

"In the kitchen." Emily made a grab for Joie's hand. "You can't go back inside."

"I have to." Joie was surprised at the strength with which the child held her arm. Finally yanking free, she made a mad dash back into the house. Smoke filled the room and if Joie hadn't been so short, she'd be inhaling the fumes. As it was, the gray cloud gagged her, bringing on a coughing fit. The haze made it impossible to locate the fire extinguisher.

She just couldn't let Matt's house burn to the ground. Closing her eyes, she remembered the four miracles left attached to her bracelet.

Joie wrapped her fingers around one. "Stop the fire!" she shouted, and the charm disappeared. Immediately, the flames went out.

Racing back outside to Emily, Joie found her sobbing, tears coursing down her cheeks leaving sooty trails on her face. "Daddy is going to be so mad."

Smoke still poured out the door and rose into the evening sky. "Don't worry, I put the fire out. It's going to be alright."

A man walking his dog stopped. "Are you girls okay?"

Emily nodded and pointed to Joie. "She stopped the fire."

"Where's your dad?" the man asked.

"He's on a not-date." Emily looked as if she was about to be carted away and put in jail. It wasn't Emily's fault the kitchen caught on fire. Joie alone held that responsibility. If she'd just done what Matt had asked, they wouldn't be in this horrible predicament.

"A not-date? What is that?" The man eyed them both.

Joie bit her lip before answering. "It's where a woman insists on going out for a drink. The man agrees. And hopefully, they find enough interest in each other that he asks her out on a real date."

"Who's babysitting you?" The man glanced between the two of them waiting for an answer.

"Um..." Joie didn't dare tell him it was her. Yet if she didn't come up with a plausible answer, he could report Matthew to the authorities for child neglect, and endangerment. He'd end up in prison, his daughter in foster care. "She ran to call the fire department. She told us to wait right here."

"I better put a call in as well."

Fear etched Emily's face and the tears increased as she grabbed ahold of Joie's hand. "You shouldn't tell lies. Daddy says it always gets you into trouble."

Joie put her hands on Emily's clasped ones. "But if I tell him the truth, he'll never believe I'm an elf. Look at what I had to do to convince your dad."

"What will we do when the pretend babysitter doesn't come back?"

Emily had a point. Joie had to think fast. With a quick glance down at her bracelet, she knew what she had to do. "I have to use the bathroom." She danced from foot to foot as she'd seen children do.

"We can't have you wet your pants, can we?" The man motioned for the girls to follow him.

"I'm not supposed to go into strangers' houses." Joie stopped dancing. "I can go behind a bush."

The man shook his head. "Okay, but don't take too long."

Joie dashed off to a bush next to the neighbor's house. Once hidden from view, she wrapped her fingers around the second charm and made her wish. "Make me a human." The charm disappeared as sparkles around her shot off in several directions. She thought for sure the lights would draw attention.

Her arms and legs grew longer, her hair darker, and her...oh, no! Her chest popped out of her blouse exposing way too much of her bare skin. She could never come back wearing the same outfit, especially one that didn't even fit. Joie had no choice but to use another one of her miracles.

Before she thought about the current fashion trends of the era, she pictured Cinderella. Now that was one girl who knew how to wear a ball gown. She gripped the miracle and made her wish.

A siren wailed from down the street, the sound getting louder the closer it got. Joie stepped from the bush, brushing at her gown as the fire engine pulled around the corner and stopped in front of the house.

Several fire fighters leapt from the truck and zipped past her with a hose to attach to the hydrant in front of the house next door. Another man held a radio to his mouth. "Engine one is on the scene of a two-story, single family residence with smoke coming from the front door, 2215 Blessing Street. Smoke alarm still sounding. Unable to tell if there are any occupants still inside."

Joie touched his elbow. "No one else is inside."

The fireman turned to Joie, eyeing her from head to toe. "Are you the home owner?"

Perhaps she'd overdone her outfit. Joie shook her head. "I'm the babysitter." She pointed at Emily. "We were making cookies and the stovetop caught fire."

"Joie?" Emily mouthed.

Joie nodded.

The chief eyed her dubiously. "You were baking in that?"

"We were...uh..."

"Playing dress up, too," Emily interjected.

He raised an eyebrow before turning back to his team. "Possible grease fire in the kitchen, use the foam as well," he yelled.

They dragged the hose toward the front door.

"Wait!" Joie called and stumbled after him, nearly tripping on the hem of her gown. "I put the fire out. We just couldn't stay inside with all the smoke."

The fire chief nodded. "She says it's already been extinguished. Make sure."

The men continued into the house, the hose snaking behind them.

"Has the owner been notified?" the fire chief asked.

"Not yet." She bent down until she was level with Emily. "It's okay – Auntie Joie is here. We'll call your dad and let him know."

The man with the dog eyed Joie for a moment before looking back to the bush. "Where's the other young'un?"

Joie straightened back up. "She...uh...ran on home."

The firefighters exited the house dragging the hose behind them. The shorter one took it to the truck and wound it back up. The other reported to the chief. "Fire's out, but there's lots of smoke still inside. We opened the windows on the lower floor. Should clear out in a bit. It'll probably smell pretty bad for a while."

"Now, let's call the owner." The chief handed the phone to Joie.

CHAPTER FIFTEEN

Matt cut another chunk off his steak, bigger than he should have, and stuffed it in his mouth. He had to get this food down fast. It had already been an hour. Clara had hardly started on her plate. Her mouth did not stop yammering.

"It was the funniest thing you've ever seen. Twice I had to tell the mother that lice nits in her hair still meant she was contagious." Clara punctuated the air with her fork.

The last thing Matt wanted to talk about over steak was bugs in the hair. Not that he was squeamish, just that his mother had taught him some things should not be discussed over meals. It never failed, though, either he or his brothers brought up poop. His mom would slam her fist on the table, pick up her plate and go into the other room to eat. Matt chuckled at the memory.

"It was hilarious." Clara took a nibble off her steak.

"Oh, no." Matt drew a somber expression across his face.

She reached across the table and laid her hand on his, intertwining her fingers with his. If she hadn't had such a firm grip, he'd have pulled away. Before he could figure out how to extricate himself, he glanced toward the door. Miss Hall entered with another woman who looked like an older version of Miss Hall. Must be her mother, or a much older sister. Their eyes met for a moment and her mouth turned down into a grimace. She leaned into the woman and whispered something. The older woman locked eyes with Matt and smiled broadly before turning back to the hostess.

Clara leaned forward, her hand still locked with Matt's. "That's Dawnetta Hall. She teaches fifth grade. And I hear she's engaged." The last bit of information sounded as though Clara had dill pickles stuck in her mouth.

Matt turned back to Clara as the hostess escorted the women to a table next to the booth where they sat.

"Hello, Clara." Miss Hall stood next to the booth while the older woman sat. She turned to Matt. "Thank you for your help with the tire this afternoon." She held out her hand. "I didn't get your name."

Matt couldn't believe this was the same harsh woman who'd practically wrestled the tire from him only hours ago. He managed to get his hand away from Clara's, stood, and held it out to the fifth grade teacher with the enchanting smile, deep green eyes and platinum blond hair. "Matthew Adams. Call me Matt."

Clara leaned back in her chair and dabbed at the corner of her mouth. "So when is your wedding again? I'll bet you're so excited."

Color rose in Dawnetta's face. "I called it off. I can't have an overseas relationship." Without elaborating, she turned to the woman with her. "This is my mother, Becky Ann Hall."

Mrs. Hall nodded. "Dawnetta told me all about your gallant rescue."

"Was nothing." Matt tipped his head in acknowledgement. "Actually, Miss Hall had it quite under control. I'm afraid I may have made it worse." Matt took a quick glance back at Clara and swallowed. He knew that look – daggers, jealousy, that thing girls do when they already have their meat hooks into a man.

"See you tomorrow morning." Clara turned her back on the pair and motioned for Matt to returned to his seat.

His cell phone vibrated. Matt checked his caller ID. Jack, his neighbor next door. Either he was walking his dog and noted something needing attention – he was notorious for making sure everyone on the block met certain criteria for the perfect neighborhood, or – Matt swallowed – the girls had gotten themselves into trouble. Leaving two children that age home alone was not going to bode well for him.

Matt answered the phone, trying not to let his voice tremble. "Hey, Jack, what's up?"

"There's been a fire at your house. Your daughter is fine. She's in good hands with your babysitter."

"Babysitter?"

Jack cleared his throat. "You did leave them with Joie, right?"

"Oh, oh, yes. I did. May I speak with her?" Matt ran a sweaty palm down the side of his pants. Child Protective Services would show up any minute and then his daughter would be gone.

"Hi, Matt. It's Joie."

It didn't sound like her. This was the voice of a grown woman. "Where's Joie?"

"Speaking." She practically bubbled. "I know you said not to let the girls do anything except watch the television. But, well, you know how my sister can be sometimes. Always wanting to make cookies. And Emily encouraged her. So we set about making gingerbread." The babysitter giggled just like Joie. It couldn't be her.

"I'll be right there." He clicked end, grabbed his jacket and shrugged. "I have an emergency."

Clara set her fork down, a grimace creasing her forehead. "I'm sorry to hear it. Anything I can do to help?"

Matt threw a wad of cash on the table "This should cover it." He didn't wait for her reply as he tugged his jacket on. He gave a quick glance at Miss Hall. Amusement spread across her face. Not daring to figure out the meaning, he fled out the door and raced to his truck.

CHAPTER SIXTEEN

Matt brought his truck to a screeching halt, barely putting it in park before he jumped out. He hit the driveway with both feet and ran to his daughter. Emily in her wheelchair next to...he gulped. It couldn't be Joie. Her hair had turned a shimmering shade of dark brown; her upturned nose still gave her a childish look. Her mouth told a different story. Gone was the impish smile, in its place, full, luscious, kissable lips turned up at the corners. He tried to keep his eyes on her face, but couldn't help but wander the full length of her. This was no elf or child. Her beauty left him stunned.

"Hi, Matt." She gave him a sheepish grin. "I know you told us not to do anything but sit and watch movies."

His eyes snapped back up to her face. "What happened?"

"Gingerbread cookies?" She pulled her mouth into a pout. "You shouldn't have left those papers so close to the stove."

"What papers? I'm never so careless." Matt furrowed his brows. He'd always been so careful about keeping things away from the stove for that very reason.

"When I turned around, some papers were burning and the fire was heading up the wall." Joie took her lower lip, a bright shade of pink, between her teeth.

The fire chief cleared his throat. "Thanks for getting here so fast. I'm Captain Landry."

Matt turned his attention to Landry. He'd deal with Joie in a moment. "Is it safe to go back inside?"

"I'd probably wait until morning. There's still a lot of smoke." Landry pulled a paper from his clipboard and handed it to Matt. "These are some things you should know before you go back inside."

Matt took the sheet and gave it a quick glance. It was hard to read much in the dark. "Thanks."

"One other thing, you can contact the Red Cross or the Salvation Army. They can help you find a place to stay and can help you with some food and clothing. That is, if you don't have any relatives you can stay with." The chief strode to the fire engine. Before he climbed in, he turned back to Matt. "You'll want to contact your insurance company in the morning."

After the emergency vehicles departed, Matt stood looking at more than half the neighborhood standing in the street and lining the sidewalk. He wasn't sure if they were gaping at the house or at the woman clad in an ice blue ball gown covered in sparkles and a tiara adorning her hair.

"Dad?" Emily tugged on his pant leg.

Matt's focus left the gawkers and turned to his daughter. "What is it, sugar?"

"Where are we going to live?" Her eyes looked up at him with moisture rimming her lashes.

He squatted down beside her. "In our house, of course."

"But what about tonight?" Emily drew her eyebrows together. "Because that fireman said we shouldn't." Suddenly her eyes brightened. "Can we stay at Miracle Inn?"

"I don't know." The week before Cadence was killed, the owners had asked him to give a bid to repair the flooded cellar. Cadence and

Emily had trailed along, with his wife telling animated stories about the only hotel in the area. Ever since then, Emily had taken to the notion of staying there.

"Please, Daddy." Emily clasped her hands in front of her. "Mommy would want us to."

Joie clasped her hands over her stomach. "You should do the things that would have brought joy to your family. It will remind you of the good things you had." Her eyes reflected the same excitement as his daughter.

With these two, he'd never see his way out of it. Matt pinched his lips together. "All right. But just for tonight."

Emily's eyes grew wide and she practically jumped out of her chair. "Where will Joie stay?"

Matt looked at Joie. "I suppose she'll stay wherever it is she goes when she's not with us."

Joie gasped and shook her head. "I can't use my magic now that I'm human."

Emily tugged on Matt's hand. "I know! She can come with us and stay in the hotel, too."

Joie shouldn't be his responsibility...maybe Mrs. Claus could just come and get her or summon her back. He had forgotten about his neighbors until Jack tapped Matt on the shoulder. "Doesn't she have her own house?"

"Oh, yes, right..." Matt fumbled for the words. "She lives..." He turned back to some of his other neighbors, avoiding Jack's glaring accusation.

Mrs. Davis stepped forward. "I have a spare room you and Emily can stay in." She shot Joie a look that declared his scandalous intentions would not be tolerated in her home. She clearly looked like she had it in mind to spread rumors the minute she left.

"Thanks, but I should have taken Emily to Miracle Inn a long time ago." He turned to Joie, and he hoped she saw the pleading in his eyes. "I'm sure Joie's family is already worried about her.

"Nah, they know where I am and want me to help out." The innocence written across Joie's face was not obvious to the spectators.

Mr. Humphrey cleared his throat. "Do you need a change of clothes? My granddaughter is about Emily's size."

Matt shook his head. "Thanks, but I can probably run inside and gather a few things."

Jack nodded to Matt's house. "I can be over first thing in the morning to help."

All of a sudden, his neighbors were a plethora of help, like they had when Cadence died. "I got it under control." He waved off their kind gestures, just like he had before.

Joie touched his arm. "People are always so much nicer around Christmas." She let out a sigh. "You should let them help you. It's good for neighbors to connect. It's what brings communities together, makes them feel like they're wanted and needed."

Matt scowled at her. If she had just done what he'd asked her to do, there'd be no need for all this community oneness. He scratched the back of his neck. His gaze rested on her full lips, drawn into a delicious curve. Matt wasn't sure where that thought had come from. Her eyes sparkled, but it wasn't from her previous mischievousness. The deep blue of her scrutiny pierced his soul as if she could read his thoughts. Pulling his eyes from her, he turned back to Mrs. Davis and Mr. Humphrey. "Thank you kindly for your offers. The damage is minimal." Then to Jack he added, "And cleanup shouldn't take long."

"I'll be over in the morning anyhow to see what you need." Jack yanked on his dog's collar and headed on up the sidewalk.

"But not too early," Matt shouted at him. "Some people like to sleep in on the weekends."

Most of the other on lookers had dispersed leaving Emily and Joie to stare at the house.

"Do you have *anything* else to wear?" Matt eyed the elf where she stood in her gown and squinted – was she wearing glass slippers?

Confusion spread across her face. “Uh, well…no. I didn’t pack any human clothes.”

Matt rolled his eyes. How in the world could she have baked cookies in that get up?

CHAPTER SEVENTEEN

When the last of the emergency vehicles had left, so had the spectators, leaving Joie, Matt, and Emily on the sidewalk. Joie brushed the skirt of her dress. She wished she'd thought through her clothing plan before she turned into a human. Cinderella's ball gown was not her best choice. She couldn't help it. Panic had taken over and this – she looked down at her dress – was the first thing that popped into her head. If she'd had time to think about it, she might have chosen something more serviceable. She drew her eyebrows together and twitched her mouth to one side in a half smile and looked up at Matt. "I'm sorry."

"Well, you should be. You've gotten me into quite a dilemma." Matt ran his hand through his hair.

Not only had she made a mess of everything, she'd ruined his chances with Ms. Evans. This feeling inside her was unlike anything she'd ever experienced before. What was it called? Guilt? The whole kitchen fire replayed over and over in her mind like a rerun of that dreadful movie she and Emily should have been watching. She'd give anything to go back and fix what had happened. Even if she could have, Joie only had one miracle left and it probably wouldn't be enough to fix all of her mistakes. No, she'd better save the last one for a real emergency.

Matt stopped pacing. "You can't go parading around in that." He motioned to her dress. "You're a little smaller than my wife." He eyed her again from head to toe.

Joie crossed her arms over her chest, uncomfortable that her breasts were now several times larger than when she'd been an elf, and her hips were much – much wider. It didn't help that Matt kept staring at her like she'd sprout other...parts of....Was he staring at her mouth? She reached up and touched her lips. Yup, those were bigger, fuller, as well.

Matt ducked his head and stared at her feet. Joie bent to look at her shoes. Oh, my! How did her feet get so far down there?

He cleared his throat. "I'm gonna see if I can find something that might fit." He left her standing on the front walk and entered the house.

Emily tugged on Joie's dress. "Didn't the fireman say that Daddy shouldn't go back into the house until tomorrow?"

"I'm sure he'll be just fine. That miracle I used on the fire probably won't cause the smoke to damage things inside."

Emily's face brightened. "You're really pretty as a lady-person, Joie."

"I am?" Joie chewed on the inside of her mouth.

"You look just like the Cinderella at Disney World, except with dark hair." Emily grabbed a fist full of Joie's dress and lifted the edge of the gown. "Look, you even have her glass slippers."

"Not very practical, huh?" Joie smoothed the skirt, the fabric rustling as if tossed by the breeze.

"But very pretty." She giggled. "I hope my dad finds somebody as nice as you." The corners of her mouth turned into a pout. "Is Santa Claus going to be angry with you when he sees you're not an elf anymore?"

Joie hadn't thought about that. She wasn't even sure if Santa would let her back into the North Pole Kingdom now that she was a human. "I don't know, sweetie."

Matt came down the walk carrying a box. A pair of sneakers dangled by their laces from his fingers. "We could probably stay in the house tonight. There's really not all that much damage and the smoke has already dissipated."

"That's because of the miracle I used." Joie eyed the box in Matt's arms.

Matt nodded and glanced back at the house.

Emily pouted. "But Daddy, you said we could stay at the inn tonight."

"You did promise," Joie nodded and held out her hand to Emily.

Emily took Joie's hand, still watching her father. "Please?"

He paused for a moment and shot a glance between the two. "All right." Matt gave an audible sigh, then took the clothes to the truck and tossed them in the back seat. Joie thought he mumbled something about what other people might say. "Let's go, ladies." He motioned for them to get in the truck.

Emily propelled her wheelchair down the walk. Joie followed behind, her glass slippers clinking on the cement. Just as she reached the truck, her ankle twisted in a dip in the ground, throwing her off balance. Her arms flailed trying to regain herself. Matt's hands went around her waist. Strong arms held her against his firm chest. He smelled nice. Why hadn't she noticed this before? Shocked, she stared up into his blue eyes, so much closer to her own now that she was a human.

His gaze locked on hers for a moment before he cleared his throat and helped her stand. "I think you should get those glass slippers off before you break your neck."

He opened the front passenger door, took her by her waist and lifted her into the truck. Then he took Emily from her wheelchair and placed her in the booster seat before buckling her in. Turning back to

Joie, he knelt next to the truck. "Give me your foot." He removed first one slipper, then the next. The feel of his hand on her bare foot sent shivers up her spine. The only time she'd experienced a sensation like that was when she forgot to wrap herself in Christmas warmth. This was a different kind of awareness. Humans had all kinds of feelings she'd never experienced as an elf.

From the back seat, Emily spoke, "Prince Charming is supposed to put the glass slipper on Cinderella's foot. Not take it off."

"I'm not Prince Charming. If she keeps tripping in these, she'll probably end up breaking them or her neck."

Emily giggled. "Silly Daddy. Cinderella's shoes are magic. They won't break."

"But I might." Joie brought her feet back into the car.

Matt reached over the back seat, brushing his arm across her neck, making her head swim with the nearness of him. What was going on with her emotions? They both exhilarated and terrified her. He handed her the tennis shoes and a pair of socks. "I don't know if they'll magically fit you or not, but at least they'll keep your feet warm."

Joie drew her legs up to her chest in an attempt to get her feet closer to her hands. All the frills of the dress and her new shape made it hard to reach them. Heat rose to her cheeks. "I'm surprised you still have Cadence's clothes."

"I gave most everything away." His voice became thick with emotion. "I only kept a few of my favorites."

"That's really sweet." Joie touched his shoulder.

"Here let me help you." He took Joie's foot, touching her bare skin again as he slipped the socks over her toes and slid them up to her ankle.

Heightened awareness of the intimate gesture sent an unexpected shiver of pleasure through her. "You kept her socks, too?"

"No, these are Emily's. They'll stretch just fine." He gave her ankle a pat after he tied the laces on her shoes.

"I could have done that." Joie flung her dress down, embarrassed at the nearness of him and then crossed her arms over her chest.

The gesture had not gone unnoticed on Matt. "I guess your body is...not what you're used to."

Joie turned her head, hoping he didn't notice how uncomfortable she felt in her new shape.

CHAPTER
EIGHTEEN

When Emily's dad wheeled her into Joie's room at the Inn, she shouted with excitement, "It's so pretty." Two antique beds with spindles sat side by side. A hurricane lamp with a doily underneath accented the period night stand.

Matt took the box of Cadence's clothes from Emily's lap and set it on one of the beds. "There are probably more clothes than you need."

Joie stood in the middle of the room. "Matt, I..."

He didn't want to hear her apologize one more time. "Emily and I will be right next door, if you need anything."

"Can we finish watching the movie?" Emily asked when Matt turned her around and pushed her toward the door.

"No, ma'am!" Normally, that face could get him to cave. However, with the fire, the Cinderella woman staring at him with those wide blue eyes, and his frustrating not-date with Clara, he had no intention of giving into pouty expressions or mischievous glances. "You two have already caused enough trouble for one day."

Joie stared at the floor. "I'm really sorry."

"Just go to bed, and we'll figure out what to do tomorrow." He probably shouldn't be telling an adult what to do. He cast her a sideways glance. "I mean. If you want to stay up, that's fine."

Joie went to Emily. "Your dad's right. We do need to get to sleep."

Emily perked up, not looking tired at all. "We *are* still going to get a Christmas tree tomorrow and decorate it just like when Mommy was alive, right?"

"We never discussed getting a tree." Matt looked between the two connivers.

Emily turned a mischievous glance at Joie. "She said we should get one."

"She did, huh?" Matt's gaze rested on Joie's soft smile. He had no idea how he'd cope with what had been Cadence's tradition.

Joie's voice came out soft, apologetic. "You can't have Christmas without a tree."

He probably should have put one up last year. His mother had suggested it, but he just hadn't had the heart to try and decorate one like his wife would have. He didn't know if he could face another year without her. "We'll see."

Emily's lower lip protruded. "You always say that when you don't want to."

Matt ran his hand through his hair. "All right, we'll get a tree."

Emily clapped her hands with glee, while Joie smiled.

"Now let's get you to bed. It's been a very..." How could Matt even describe today? All of it because of the appearance of one meddling elf. "I'm going to bed." Pushing Emily's chair, he headed toward his room. Before opening the connecting door, he said, "If you need anything, I'm right through here."

"Okay," she said.

After closing the door behind him, he lifted Emily from the chair and set her on the bed.

"Daddy?"

"Hmm..."

She peeled her shirt off and tossed it to Matt. "Joie's super nice, huh?"

Matt shook his head and retrieved her nightgown. "She's meddlesome is what she is."

"I hope she finds someone nice, too...by Christmas."

He tried to hold back a chuckle. "You do realize Christmas is in five days, don't you?"

Emily held up her arms for him to put her nightgown on. "She can use magic and stuff."

"Five days is too short of a time to find true love." It had taken him a very long time to find Cadence, never mind that he'd known her since elementary school.

"But Dad, Mrs. Claus wouldn't have sent Joie if she couldn't do it."

Heavens, his daughter could be pushy. "Nevertheless, I'm the one who decides if I want you to have another mommy."

Tears sprang to his daughter's eyes and trickled down her cheeks. "I want my mommy."

"I know, baby." He pulled her onto his lap and tucked her head under his chin. "I want your mommy, too." His heart tightened into a knot and he wondered if anyone could ever untie it. "What if Joie doesn't find someone I can love? We're okay, just the two of us, huh?"

Emily's head shook from side to side and gentle sobs quavered her body. "I'm the only girl in my whole school who doesn't have a mommy."

Probably not the only girl, but felt like it, he was sure. Maybe it was time to start looking. And not just the blind dates set up for him in the last few months. He'd make a bigger effort to find the one who would make both Emily and him happy.

He glanced at the connecting door for a moment, thinking about Joie's attempt to set him up. His date with Clara had been a disaster. That hadn't entirely been Joie's fault since it was doomed from the beginning. Maybe he should thank Joie for ending it early.

Matt stroked her hair. "Sweetheart, finding a mother for you means I have to really like her, because we'd be stuck with her if she turned out to be the wrong choice."

"Ms. Evans is nice."

Matt tickled her arm when she flopped it on his knee. "Yes, she is and she would be a good mommy to you. But, honey, she's not right for me."

Emily yawned. "What about Miss Hall?"

"We'll see."

She jerked her hand away and tucked it under her pillow. "That means no."

Matt pinched his lips together. He hadn't realized that every time he said that, it did mean he didn't want to. "I'll ask her out on a date, okay? And then we'll just see how it goes from there, alright?"

"Okay, Daddy." Emily closed her eyes and Matt turned the switch on the table lamp, sending the room into semi-darkness, the bathroom light casting a sliver of yellow across the carpet.

Matt tucked the blankets around her, kissed her on the forehead and went to his bed. He stared at the connecting door. Maybe all he'd needed was a gentle push to start dating again. He shook his head... Joie had hardly been gentle.

What was he thinking, letting Joie stay here in the hotel with him? He should have sent her back to the North Pole where she belonged. The rumors would surely fly, especially after what he'd told the neighbors about her. Now this finding a wife and the whole Christmas tree business....

With a resigned sigh, Matt crossed to the window and stared out at the wet pavement. The rain fell with a vengeance; the homes across the street were watery mists of their brick selves. At least, the clouds had held back until they'd checked into the hotel. He hoped tomorrow's forecast of clear skies held true since he really didn't want to have to deal with repairs on top of the rain.

Movement from behind one of the tall elms brought Matt squinting into the night. Had he seen another child outside in the freezing cold? Perhaps he should go check and make sure. This was no time of night to be without supervision, especially in the cold conditions. He searched for a moment longer, hoping adults would show up to take care of the kid.

Checking again, Matt lost sight of the child. Maybe he'd ducked behind a tree.

A soft tapping on his door took his attention from the window.

Annoyed, Matt answered the door. "Now what's wrong?"

"I'm sorry to bother you." Joie had changed into a pair of skinny jeans and snug shirt, her graceful curves accentuating her womanly figure. His heart rate ramped up and his empty stomach fluttered. Cadence's clothes fit Joie better than they'd fit his wife.

"Um...." She clasped her hands together and her face displayed as much displeasure as he himself felt.

"What's wrong now?" Matt whispered and took a quick peek over his shoulder.

"I have to leave for a few minutes. You wouldn't happen to have an umbrella?" Joie took the corner of her lower lip in her teeth.

"There's one in the truck, but I think you'll probably end up soggy before you reach it."

"Oh." She backed into her room. "Never mind then. I'll just have to meet him in the lobby." Joie sat on the edge of the bed and pulled his wife's tennis shoes back on.

Emily propped herself up on one elbow. "Can I come, too?"

Matt blew out a huff of air and crossed the room. "You, my dear child, are going to go to sleep. I think you've had enough excitement for one day."

Emily looked up at him. "Do you think Joie has a boyfriend elf, or maybe a husband elf?"

"I have no idea." He tucked the covers around her.

Joie's face had turned a vibrant shade of red. "I won't be gone long." She shrugged into one of Cadence's jackets and fled out the door.

He kissed Emily on top of her head. "I thought you were asleep."

"I'm too excited to sleep." Emily pulled her covers up to her chin. "Daddy, do you think Joie is pretty?"

"As a human?"

Emily nodded.

Matt considered his daughter's question for a moment. "I suppose so."

A serious expression creased his daughter's brow. "Do you think her boyfriend is going to be mad about her being a human?"

At that, Matt let out a chuckle. "Sweetheart, I have no idea what happens with relationships in the elf kingdom. Now go to sleep."

"Okay." Emily didn't sound like she would comply. He mentally prepared himself for the antics she went through to stay up.

Matt kissed her on the top of her head. "Goodnight." He had a hard time picturing elves with significant others. Joie had mentioned births and deaths in the elf world. "A boyfriend, huh?" He shook off the mental image as he took another peek out the window.

CHAPTER NINETEEN

Joie gripped the rail. Even though she'd navigated them going up, she didn't like the thought of tumbling down the stairs if she couldn't get control of her freakishly long legs and large feet.

Wink Everwarmth stood at the bottom of the stairs. "What in Krispy Kremes happened to you?" He put his hands on his hips and shot Joie a look of confusion.

"Why are you here?" Joie did not want to have to explain it all to Wink.

Once she reached the lobby Wink looked up at her. "Santa sent me."

"Santa doesn't even know I'm here." She towered over him like one of the giant gingerbread men guarding the entrance to North Pole Kingdom.

Wink stammered for a moment. "Well, he should know what you're up to." He gestured from the top of her head down to her toes. "And what is all this? I almost didn't recognize you."

"I had to use a couple of the miracles." She didn't dare tell him she only had one left.

The desk clerk came from the back room. "Oh, hello Miss Noel. Is this your son? I didn't see him come in with you."

Wink snapped around. "Son? Do I look like I'm related to her? She's supposed to marry me."

Joie put her hand over her heart. "Oh, children are so dear, wanting to marry their mommies and daddies." Joie took Wink's hand. "Come on, sweetheart. It's way past your bedtime."

"But – "

Before Wink could say any more, she yanked on his arm, tugging him down the hall.

The clerk pulled his eyebrows together and pointed. "Your rooms are upstairs."

"Oh, yes, you're right." Joie smiled.

"I'm not climbing those," Wink practically shouted. He'd never been one to speak quietly.

"Well, no one is going to carry you." She frowned at Wink; she could barely navigate the stairs herself. Joie leaned in close to Wink's ear. "If you don't get your little sugar plum butt up those stairs, I will not tell you what happened."

Wink yanked his hand out of hers and took exaggerated steps up the stairs.

Joie turned back to the clerk and gave him a little shrug. "You just have to know how to motivate them."

Once they reached the top of the stairs, Joie led him down the hallway and stopped in an alcove. "Look..." She tried to figure out what to tell him. They both had worked in wooden toys, and he'd been sugaring up to her for the last few months. He was nice, and funny, charming without being overbearing, cute, and she liked him, but that's where it stopped. She just didn't feel about him the way he felt about her. Joie knew they weren't meant to be. Now that she was a human, she didn't even know if she could go back to North Pole Kingdom and be with him, even if she'd want to, which she emphatically did not. With a sigh, she sat on the cushioned bench.

Wink hopped up next to her. "We'll just have Santa undo whatever miracles you messed up. I'm sure he can change you back into an elf. It's not so terrible that you messed up your assignment."

She eyed him with suspicion. "How did you know about why I'm here?"

"Why else would you be here?" Then he motioned to her from head to toe. "But this is a huge mess up. I suggest you head back to NPK immediately and have this..." again he motioned to her body. "...fixed."

Joie bit her lip. She hated to leave her assignment unfinished. She just had to find a match for Matt. She glanced down at Wink. "How did you know I was here, specifically?" Joie had thought her mission was a secret, just between her and Mrs. Claus. She hadn't expected her to tell Santa.

Wink cleared his throat. He did that when he was going to use a factlet on her. "I saw a letter sitting on Mrs. Claus's desk."

"There's lots of letters she takes care of. How did you know which one was assigned to me?" Joie narrowed her eyes at him.

He cleared his throat again. "Your name was written at the bottom."

"Really?" Another factlet. Mrs. Claus used special ink that only she could see. It kept Santa from worrying too much about requests that he might not be able to fill.

"What?" He drew his eyebrows together.

"Honestly, how did you find me?"

"I told you – "

"Wink, seriously, if you'd just tell the truth, this would be so much easier on both of us."

Wink locked his fingers together and looked down at them. "All right, fine. When I couldn't locate you anywhere in North Pole Kingdom, I just knew you were on a special assignment."

"It's my first one, so how would you know I was on an assignment?"

He continued staring down at his hands. "Well, everyone knows you're up for that big promotion. I suspected that Mrs.

Claus would send you on a mission to see if you're the right one for the job."

"That still doesn't tell me how you knew where I was." Joie shook her head.

"I told Mrs. Claus you're pregnant."

Joie stood and jammed her hands on her hips. "You what?"

"I told her you wanted an assignment so that you could run away because you were so embarrassed." He barely raised his eyes and shot her a sidelong glance.

Joie jerked her hands to her side and strode down the hall several paces before she stomped back to Wink. "And Mrs. Claus believed you?"

Wink didn't say anything for a moment. "Well, actually..."

"Actually what?"

"She didn't believe me. But she figured if I'd go to such trouble to find you, I must be crazy about you." Wink jumped off the couch and went to Joie. He took her hand in his. "I am crazy about you. I want you to come back to North Pole Kingdom and marry me."

She couldn't let Wink think that she'd actually consider it. "You are crazy. The fact is Wink, I just can't."

"Well, why not?" he yelled as hurt spread across his face.

If Wink could tell factlets to find her, then she could tell them to get rid of him. "Because I've fallen in love with someone else."

"Who?"

Before Joie could respond, Matt's door opened.

Wink's gaze fell on the handsome man standing there looking at them. "Him?"

Joie nodded and hoped Matt hadn't been listening.

CHAPTER TWENTY

Matt stared at the young man who also sported pointed ears and a red scarf. Other than that, he looked mostly like a young teenager. "Sorry, I don't want to interrupt you and your boyfriend."

The kid gave Matt one of those prepubescent eye rolls. "She's going to be my fiancé. And I'll have you know, you don't stand a chance."

Joie jumped to her feet and raced to Matt's side. With her back to the kid, she mouthed. "Pretend." At least that's what he thought she'd said.

"Now that I'm human..." She slipped her arm around Matt's waist. "I'm no longer interested in elves."

What was she talking about? Joie was supposed to find him a wife. The last thing he wanted or needed was an elf dressed up as a human. Underneath that womanly shape, and what a shape it was, beat the heart of a dear little elf, one with perhaps some peculiar ways of doing things. Not to mention the whole appearing and disappearing thing. He was not interested in Joie that way.

"You think you may have won, but I'll be back." The kid jumped off the bench, clenching his fists, then disappeared.

Matt shook his head. After Joie popping in and out, he thought it shouldn't surprise him.

Joie had kept her arm around him. He looked down at her and she jumped, extricating herself. "Sorry." She fluttered her eyelashes at him before looking down at her shoes.

"So that's your fiancé?" Matt was surprised at the warmth still lingering at his waist.

Joie let out a huff of air. "Oh, peppermint sticks! He's not my boyfriend. He's been after me for the last few months. I already told him I'm not interested. He won't take no for an answer."

An elderly couple had come up the stairs and headed toward them, stopping and smiling as they passed Matt and Joie. The cute little white-haired woman reminded her a little of Mrs. Claus. "You two look like the most adorable couple this side of Miracle. No wonder she doesn't want that other man."

Color flooded Joie's cheeks, and she went back to staring at her shoes.

The man smiled. "I'm sure glad Shirley didn't pick that other fella." He took his wife's hand and gave it a squeeze. "Why anyone can see you two are perfect for each other."

"Thank you." Matt ran his hand through his hair. He took Joie's hand, pulled her into his room, and with a sharp click, closed the door.

"Matt..." Joie hadn't released his hand. It certainly didn't feel like an elf's hand. It fit quite nicely in his.

"Hmm..." Matt kind of liked the look of confusion in her brilliant blue eyes. They contrasted nicely with the blush covering her face.

"I didn't mean..." she stammered. "I – I, uh."

"I know. You were just using me to get out of a sticky situation." Women liked to do that all the time, and somehow it always backfired.

"I've never lied before." She raised her hands to her chest. "Why does it not feel good in my heart?" She then put her fingers on her temple. "And something up here hurts. Not as in a physical hurt, but it just feels weird."

Matt turned loose of her hand and instantly missed the feel of her warmth. He went to the bathroom sink, filled a glass with some water, and brought it to her. "It's called guilt. And it hurts like all get out if you're a person who has any morals."

Joie took the glass and sipped. "I will never tell a lie again."

Matt chuckled. "You have already told several lies. One right after another, I might add."

"I did?" Joie pulled her eyebrows together. "When?"

"Let's see." He motioned to her size. "You told Jack you were Joie's big sister. That you took her home. That your mother was worried about her, and then the whole dress thing..."

"Those weren't lies." Joie's eyes widened at his accusation.

"Then what do you call them?"

"A factlet." She said it like everyone should know what it meant. "You know, like when adults tell their child it's time for bed, when really all the grown-ups want to do is have the little darling out of the way. And then, there's the one you told Emily two years ago."

"What?"

"The growing rock." Joie flashed him her familiar smile – the one that held mischief. "You told her that if she watered it and it grew, then it would turn into a princess tiara and if she put it on, she'd magically become a princess."

"Oh, that one." Matt swallowed the lump in his throat. He'd only done that to keep her from pestering him about princesses. Emily still kept the pebble in her flower pot but hadn't watered it since Cadence's death.

"Or when your wife took her to the store and she was always picking things up." Joie sipped her water.

Matt puzzled over that one. "I don't know about that lie."

Joie set the cup on the table. "She said, 'You should be petting kittens instead. If you keep touching things, it makes a kitty die because you didn't save your touches for the kitten."

He couldn't imagine his wife saying something like that to Emily. "Cadence would never have done that."

"Well, she did. And what about the time that Emily wouldn't eat her carrots?"

"If she ate enough of them, they'd start to taste like candy." Matt shook his head. "I get it." He should probably stop telling factlets.

"But what I told Wink..." Joie's face fell and she slumped into the chair. "That was a lie. And I don't like the way it makes me feel."

Matt sat in a chair opposite from where she sat. "This must be really hard to be a human."

Her nod was barely perceptible in the soft light. "I have no idea what to do. I've lost my magic; I can't go back to North Pole Kingdom unless I use this miracle." She fumbled with the charm on her bracelet.

Matt stood and crossed to Joie, then taking her hand he pulled her to stand in front of him. The softness of her hand in his, her delicate fingers resting in his, the look in her eyes, so lost and confused.... He tried to remind himself what she'd looked like before her incredible transformation. He couldn't concentrate on anything but her delectable fragrance, like fresh snow, if there was such an aroma. All he could see was an incredibly vulnerable woman, sent rolling down an avalanche of emotions.

Her gaze drifted to his face. "Matt...I..."

"What is it?"

She withdrew her hand and went to the window. "I'm having a hard time being human. It's not just the lie thing."

Matt followed her and stood next to her, waiting for her to explain. She claimed to have lost her magic, yet something was happening to him he couldn't explain. The elf forgotten, he just wanted to...even he couldn't explain it. She drew him in like a crisp fire to frostbite. Had his heart been so frozen for so long?

"I have this really weird feeling right here." She put her hand over her stomach.

"What do you mean? Are you sick? Do you feel like throwing up?" Matt took a step back, instantly regretting the distance.

"No, not really." Joie clenched her hand. "It's like when Santa tells us that we've done an exceptional job and hands us each a peppermint stick with Pop Rocks in it."

"Pop Rocks?"

Joie's eyes closed. "Except, those are magic. They flutter around in your stomach, tickling your insides and sometimes it makes you giggle."

Definitely something magical was happening to him. Matt took her shoulder and turned her to face him. "Do you feel like giggling now?"

Joie placed her other hand on top of her fist. "No. It's different, like..."

When she trailed off, he picked up one of her hands and rubbed his thumb across her skin. It was kind of fun to watch her struggle with human emotions. As a teenager, he'd experienced all kinds of feelings when he'd been around girls. The flutter of butterflies in his stomach, the racing heart. Back then, the sensations were fun. Then he'd met Cadence and everything changed. He still liked those feelings, but they grew into something deeper.

Looking down at Joie, those same sensations coursed through his body. All of a sudden he had the urge to kiss her. He bent and placed one hand around the back of her neck and drew her close. She rested her free hand on his chest; the warmth of her fingertips penetrated his shirt. Releasing his hold on her hand he put his at the small of her back, pressing her body closer.

With her eyes wide, she parted her lips in a gasp. He couldn't take his gaze off her mouth. Pop Rocks hit his stomach as well. Her sweet breath met his.

Suddenly, Emily's voice fluttered between them. "Daddy?"

CHAPTER TWENTY-ONE

Long after Joie had settled into the bed, she stared up at the ceiling. He'd almost kissed her. It sent all kinds of sensations, both frightening and amazing. She touched her lips as if trying to figure out what might have happened if he'd actually kissed her. She wished Emily hadn't interrupted them. It might have been nice to have a human kiss her.

What was she thinking? She couldn't get distracted from finding Matt a wife. Rolling onto her stomach, she had to consider what had happened, for research purposes, of course. It might help her understand what a possible wife might experience in Matt's arms.

The thought of another woman kissing Matt laid a sensation on her stomach she didn't like. One that twisted it into licorice knots, tightening her stomach until she wondered if she'd ever be able to eat again. The more she tried to ignore what it meant, the tighter it pulled at her insides.

Joie gripped the pillow. Good golly gumdrops! Mrs. Claus had sent her here on an assignment; find a mother for Emily and a wife for Matthew. Joie squelched the feelings gnawing at her insides and determined to complete her mission, return to North Pole Kingdom as fast as she could and place as much distance between her and Matt as possible. Maybe as an elf she could forget him.

It wasn't that Joie didn't like the feelings she had as a human. They were confusing. How did she account for them all – guilt, happiness, sorrow, and especially joy whenever Matthew Adams was nearby? It made her insides all fluttering and excited and peaceful all at the same time. How could that be possible?

Hopefully Mrs. Claus could explain what she was feeling, and it would make more sense. She was a human after all.

CHAPTER TWENTY-TWO

Early the next morning, Matt waited at the elevator for Joie to join him. She rounded the corner slightly out of breath, carrying the box. She'd put on the same jeans and t-shirt she'd worn last night, or maybe she'd slept in them.

"I gave you plenty to wear." Maybe later today, he'd take her to the store and get some clothes that didn't constantly remind him of his wife. He should have donated that box to the church, or at least to a thrift store. Now, here Joie was in Cadence's clothes.

"It was easier to just put these on this morning." Joie stood next to Emily and patted her arm. "How did you sleep last night?"

"Daddy snores."

Joie chuckled. "Santa snores so loud we can hear him all over North Pole Kingdom. I think he is so tired when he settles in for his long winter's nap, he just can't help it."

Matt ignored her and pushed the elevator button several times.

"Dad, it doesn't matter how many times you push, it doesn't make it come faster." Emily was starting to sound more and more grown up.

He pushed it one more time. "Maybe the elevator elves haven't awakened yet."

Joie giggled. "That's the most ridiculous thing I've ever heard. There's no such things."

Matt couldn't help it, he laughed out loud. "And I didn't believe in Santa's elves before yesterday, either."

"How come, Daddy?" Emily gazed up at him. "You used to tell me to be good because Santa's elves are always watching and reporting back to Santa."

Darn! He'd have to watch what he said around his daughter. He squatted down beside her. "Well, sweetheart, I mean, I didn't believe that Joie was an elf."

Joie leaned over so her face was close to Emily's. "Once a child reaches a certain age, they quit believing in Santa. That's when they lose the magic of Christmas."

Emily's lip protruded. "Is that what happened after Mommy died, and I got hurt?"

Matt wasn't sure how to respond. It wasn't Santa he'd quit believing in last year, it was God. A loving Heavenly Father would never have taken his wife and left his daughter confined to a wheelchair. If He was so merciful, then why did He allow bad things to happen? He stood and pressed the button again. "Looks like we'll have to take the stairs."

After scooping Emily out of her chair, he turned to Joie. "You can carry that down the stairs."

A look of fear crossed her face. "Sure." She didn't sound overly confident.

Joie shifted the box in her arm and gripped the rail. She had no idea how she would get the chair folded and down the stairs.

"I guess you've lost your elf strength." He shifted Emily in his arm and with his opposite hand, he lifted the wheelchair and descended the stairs.

Once he reached the bottom, he turned to see Joie taking the steps slowly. She reached him with a deep exhalation. “I don’t like stairs.” She took the wheelchair from him and unfolded it.

Matt set his daughter back into it and released the brake. “I’d think you’d be more comfortable with them as a human.” He studied Joie for a moment, trying to picture her as the elf who’d shocked, surprised, and scared the daylights out of him, landing him in a ditch, twice. Her frightened eyes met his. His stomach did a little flip of compassion at her expression.

Joie turned and looked back up the way she’d come. “When I look down at the bottom of the steps, it seems like such a long way to fall, and I’m just not that steady with my new body.”

Matt shook his head. He’d think that as a smaller person it would look so much farther down. “I take it there aren’t any stairs in the North Pole?”

Joie smoothed her hands over her slacks and patted her hair as if she’d messed it up traversing the steps. “Yes, but they’re elf-sized.”

Matt looked down at his daughter who had been listening quietly, her hands folded neatly in her lap. He brushed the top of her head. “Let’s go see how much damage there is.”

In no time, they reached the house. Matt parked the truck in the driveway and got out.

Joie still sat in the front seat. Was she expecting him to open her door? He probably should since his mama had taught him to be a gentleman. Emily had already unbuckled herself, waiting for him to put her in her wheelchair.

Matt retrieved the wheelchair and set it beside the truck before lifting Emily into his arms. Joie had still not moved from the truck. She sat chewing her bottom lip, fidgeting with her fingernails. Once he secured Emily, he opened the passenger side door. “Let’s go see what you two gals got yourselves into.”

Joie slipped out of the truck, her feet landing on the wet pavement. She turned to Matt. “I’m so sorry…for everything. I should have listened to you.”

"What's done is done. Luckily, I have a great insurance policy, and if I do the work myself, I'll have a little extra for presents."

"Are we going to have Christmas this year?" Emily's doubtful eyes met his.

He pushed Emily up the walk. "I suppose so." He glanced back at Joie as she trailed behind them. His statement must be the reason her face had brightened.

Other than the lingering smell of smoke and the huge, gaping hole where the fireman had punched through the wall checking for embers, the kitchen didn't look too bad. Matt pulled at the sheetrock behind the oven. With his experience in construction, he'd have everything back in shape by the end of the weekend. All he needed to do was make a quick trip to his supply yard for materials and be back in less than an hour.

Joie stood behind Emily with her hands on the wheelchair. "Can you fix it?"

"It'll be easy." Matt looked around to see how much residue he'd have to clean up. There wasn't a bit of it anywhere in the kitchen. "How did you put out the fire without an extinguisher?"

"Oh." Joie pulled her eyebrows together; a worried expression crossed her face. "I used one of the miracles Mrs. Claus gave me."

Before Matt could respond, a sharp knock sounded on the front door. Matt's mother opened it and stepped inside. "Oh, my golly, I just heard you had some trouble last night."

"Grandma!" Emily squealed and held out her arms for a hug.

His mom went to Emily in an instant, bent down, and wrapped Emily in a tight embrace. "Hello, my little pumpkin." When she stood, her gaze went from Matt to the burned wall before resting on Joie. "Who's this?"

The last thing Matt needed was to have to explain Joie and what happened. He took a deep breath and greeted her. "This is my friend, Joie. She was babysitting for me last night."

His mother looked puzzled. "Well, why was she babysitting when you could have brought Emily to me?"

"You didn't answer your phone…again."

His mother ignored his comment as her face darkened. "And why on earth did you go out with that nurse from the school? It's all over town, you know. And then shamelessly checking into a hotel with a woman. Where is your decency?"

Matt let out a huff. He had no idea how he was going to explain everything to his mother, and he certainly couldn't tell her the truth. "Suffice it to say, that I will not be going on a second date with Ms. Evans."

Emily giggled. "See, it was a date. Did you kiss her?"

Ugh! "It was not a date and I did *not* kiss her." Matt glanced at Joie then back at his mother. "I'll have you know I did not share a room with Joie; we were in separate ones." He had not meant for that to come out like that.

"Well, that won't keep anybody from thinking otherwise." She put her prim hands on her hips in a gesture Matt knew all too well. "You could have come and stayed at my place."

"Daddy promised we could stay at the hotel." Emily batted her eyelashes at her grandmother. "And Joie doesn't have anywhere else to go."

"Well, I'll have a lot of explaining to do to the church ladies." Mom turned to Joie and put out her hand. "I'm Mrs. Adams, but you can call me Flora."

Here came the part where his mother would glean whatever information she could to either push Matt into a relationship, or decide this one wasn't good enough to keep.

Joie took Flora's hand. "It's nice to meet you." Her face lit up as she shook hands with his mother. Great, just what he needed, more meddling in his love life.

"I don't know why I've never met you before." Flora smiled and flashed Matt that look; the one that said, *wait until I learn all I can.* "Where are you from?"

"North of here," Matt jumped in. "Way north. I'm sure you don't know anyone where she's from."

"Now Matthew, I think the young lady can speak for herself." Flora patted Joie's hand. "So tell me all about how you and my Matthew met."

Joie looked at the hand holding hers and then to Matt. Her eyes drifted back to his mother's face. "Well,..." Matt could tell Joie was fighting for the right words, trying to avoid telling a lie.

Before one could escape her lips, Emily tugged on her grandmother's shirt tail. "She's going to help Daddy find a mommy for me."

Mom's eyes lingered on Joie's for a moment longer before turning to Emily. "Is she now?" She had not turned loose of Joie's hand. "How is she going to do that?"

Emily's eyes grew wide with excitement. "She's an elf from the North Pole and has all kinds of magic spells she can use."

Matt wanted to disappear into the floor.

Mom turned back to Joie. "Well, now, that would be something if you could magically find a mother for my granddaughter." Her gaze shifted to Matt. "And that would mean a wife for you."

"Now, Mom, I don't need the three of you meddling in my affairs of the heart." Matt had to get his mother out of the house. This would go from bad to worse in no time at all. The last thing he wanted or needed was to be hitched to an elf, even if she'd become human.

Joie smiled and put her other hand over the top of Flora's. "You know, sometimes things aren't always what they appear."

"I like you, Miss..."

"Noel."

"Joie Noel. You must have been born on Christmas day for your parents to name you that." Mom turned to Matt again. "You should have told me about this dear girl."

Emily tugged on Flora's blouse again. "She really is an elf."

A look of wicked mischief crossed Flora's face as she studied Joie. "Well, if you can do what the rest of us have failed to do since Cadence's death, then more power to you."

"Now, Mom. I'm sure I can handle my own love life."

Mom shook her head. Here it came. "Now, Matthew Adams, if your brother hadn't set you up on that date with Cadence, you'd still be the loneliest bachelor in all of Texas." She placed her hand on Emily's shoulder. "And I would have never gotten this adorable young lady as my granddaughter."

Joie's eyes widened. "You needed help finding your first wife, too?"

Mom linked arms with Joie, a sly look in her eyes. "Finding a date to prom, the church mix and mingle when he came home from college. It seems this boy – "

"Man." Matt gave a huff. Why did his mother insist that he'd never grown up? In her eyes he'd always be twelve.

"Man." His mom gave a slight shake of her head and turned back to Joie. "Now then, how do you propose to find a wife for my son?"

Matthew gulped. His mother was on a mission and if he wasn't careful, he'd be walking down the aisle with Joie.

CHAPTER TWENTY-THREE

Joie liked Mrs. Adams. She could tell in an instant that Matthew's mother would be a great ally in finding just the right wife for him. She smiled at Mrs. Adams. "So, tell me how his brother managed to find Matt's first wife."

Mrs. Adams pulled Joie out of the kitchen. "Actually, Matthew and Cadence had known each other since elementary school. She was in Todd's class. Those kids went through junior high and high school together."

"Who's Todd?" Joie asked.

"That's Matt's younger brother."

Matt had not followed them into the living room. Joie looked over her shoulder to see where he'd gone. His arms crossed, he leaned against the counter, a deep scowl across his face. This must be painful for him to hear. She shook her head and shot him what she hoped was a look of compassion. Joie loved hearing *how we met* stories. In spite of the disgruntled look on Matt's face, Joie wanted Mrs. Adams to continue. "That's a long time to get to know someone pretty well. You said that Todd introduced them."

"That's where the story takes a really fun turn." A smile deepened the slight wrinkles at Mrs. Adams's eyes.

"I like this part," Emily said.

Mrs. Adams stroked Emily's cheek. "Cadence was...shall we say a bit of a butterball all through school. She was a pretty enough girl, but no one seemed to pay much attention to her."

"Some people can be so judgmental." Joie hated that people's acceptance of each other more often than not rested on outward appearance.

"Yes they can. And my Matthew was no different." Mrs. Adams gave a light huff. "I knew that deep down inside that young lady beat a heart of pure gold. She was kind, and generous, and loving. Todd and Cadence were playmates and then best friends in high school."

Joie pulled her eyebrows together. "Then why didn't she and Todd get married?"

Mrs. Adams gave a little laugh. "Oh, they might have, if his heart wasn't already set on someone else. And everyone could see that Cadence had eyes for Matt. Sometimes I think she was only friends with Todd just so she could come to the house and be around Matt."

Little butterflies tickled Joie's insides. She hoped one day to feel that way over a man. Her thoughts came to a screeching halt. Where did that notion come from? She meant elf? Yes, an elf who would make her immensely happy. A man. Hershey nuggets, what was she thinking? "Go on, how did they finally get together?"

A soft expression crossed her face as if Mrs. Adams was reliving the event. "Matthew had been away to college for several years and hadn't come home much during that time. Hannah, his sister, passed away just before Matthew graduated."

"Oh, that's so sad." Joie couldn't imagine the pain of losing a child.

"It was a hard time for all of us, but not unexpected." Mrs. Adams led Joie to the couch and patted the seat next to her. "Cancer."

Joie nodded her head. "We have that where I'm from, too."

Mrs. Adams shot her a puzzled look but continued with her story. "At the viewing, Todd introduced Cadence to him."

"But I thought they went to school together. Why wouldn't Matt know her?"

Matt slammed something in the kitchen, a pot probably. Mrs. Adams leaned in close and lowered her voice. "Because he didn't recognize her. She'd slimmed down a lot, learned how to do her hair and make-up." She chuckled softly. "I always saw the beauty in her before that."

Joie nodded. "He did see her inner beauty, too, didn't he?"

"Yes, he did." A soft smile spread across her face as if trying to cover the sadness in her eyes.

Matt burst from the kitchen and headed toward the front door. "And the rest was history. We got married, had a pretty little baby, until some moron who decided to text and drive ended our happily ever after." He stormed out of the house, slamming the door behind him.

"He's never quite gotten over Cadence's death." Mrs. Adams let out a breath of air.

No one ever got over someone's death, especially if that person was loved. "You're right. But at some point you have to get used to living without that person in your life."

Mrs. Adams nodded. "And he hasn't gotten used to that, either." Mrs. Adams patted Joie's hand, stood and followed Matt out.

Emily had sat quietly listening. "He doesn't like to talk about Mommy."

"I can imagine." Joie bit her lip. The sooner she found someone for Matt to fall in love with, the sooner he'd be able to move on with his life. Again, that odd sensation welled up in her heart, a most unpleasant one. Why did it do that every time she thought about Matt finding a wife? She didn't dare ask Matt what it meant.

CHAPTER TWENTY-FOUR

Before Matt had the car running, his mother came down the driveway. He didn't want to talk to anyone at the moment, especially not about Cadence. She'd been the center of his world. If only he'd paid more attention to her in high school, married her before he'd gone off to college and taken her out of Miracle, Texas, his wife would still be alive and his daughter wouldn't be trapped in a wheelchair. That woman would have never caused the accident that killed his wife.

Mom opened the door and climbed in beside her son. "I know you're hurting. It's how I felt when your father died."

"You had Dad a whole lot longer than I had Cadence." God had ripped Cadence from him too soon. They had dreamed of making his company expand so they could have a bigger house to fill with more kids, then growing old together.

"Who knows why some people are taken sooner than later?" Mom tried to put her hand on his arm, but he pulled it away.

"I know why she was taken. Because Laura Milo thought it was okay to text and drive." Stupid people checking their cell phones caused so much grief and pain. That woman was a grown-up. She should have known better.

Mom had dropped her hand back in her lap. "The only way for you to find peace and move forward is for you to forgive her."

"She killed my wife. She doesn't deserve it." Matt gripped the steering wheel.

"It doesn't matter whether she deserves it or not. You're the one that is being eaten up by hanging on to blaming that poor woman."

He didn't want to talk about Laura Milo. Turning to face his mother he said, "I'm going to go to the lumber yard to get some materials. If you don't want to go along, then I suggest now would be a good time to get out of the truck. Otherwise, you'll be listening to a whole lot of silence."

Mom opened the door and slid out. "If you had any sense at all, you'd invite that delightful woman to join you. I'll stay and watch Emily."

"Now why would I take Joie with me?" He couldn't believe his mother would throw them together.

Mom stood beside the open door. "Because she's a sweet and thoughtful woman. She says she's here to find you a wife. Well, if you'd take a serious look at what's right in front of you, you'd stop looking elfwhere."

"Elfwhere?"

"I said, elsewhere." Mom added under her breath, "Not that you've been looking anywhere."

"Joie is an elf all the way from the North Pole." The words flew out of his mouth before he could stop them.

"Elf, angel. It doesn't matter. I can sense she is goodness to the bone. I can tell Emily adores her, and she's a pretty good judge of character." Mom narrowed her eyes. "I'll go get her and the two of you get what you need to patch things up. I'll watch Emily."

Ugh. He hated that his mother could be so insistent, nosy, and down-right meddling. He couldn't figure out why the idea that her son believed Joie was an elf escaped him. Surely she wouldn't suggest a relationship with someone who had identity issues. Never mind that Matt knew she was an elf. But his mother had only known Joie less than a half hour and already considered Joie a prospect. For all Mom knew, Joie could have escaped the looney bin and was on the lam avoiding the men in white jackets. If he hung around Joie much longer, he might find himself in the same situation.

Speaking of the nut-case elf, she stood at the door, with his mom helping her into a jacket. Something about the way his mother leaned in close to Joie's ear made him nervous. What advice could she possibly be giving Joie?

Joie nodded and gave his mother a quick hug before hurrying to the truck. A slight drizzle picked up again, making the pavement slippery. He should probably get out and help her so she didn't fall. Matt supposed that not only was she not used to the rain, preferring snow, she was unaccustomed to her new height. That had to be something to contend with, especially with the sloping driveway.

With a sigh, Matt climbed out of the truck and into the frigid air.

"Here, let me help you." Matt took her by the elbow and steadied her as they made their way to the truck.

"You really want me to go with you?" Joie's surprise hung thick in her voice.

Mom stood at the doorway with her eyebrows raised. Was that a factlet or lie that Mom had told to convince Joie to go with him? Either way, Matt suspected their trip to the lumber yard would be anything but uneventful.

CHAPTER
TWENTY-FIVE

Joie could not contain her joy at being with Matt again. Even if they didn't run into any eligible ladies for Matt, she could spend more time with him, getting to know what he liked, what he found attractive in a woman. Besides, she liked being with him. Not that she could explain why. He was often surly and doubtful.

Glancing over at him, she wished she could read his thoughts. He'd been awfully quiet the whole drive. Maybe it was best to leave him alone in his thoughts for a while.

Once they reached the lumber yard, Joie didn't wait for him to open her door, but hopped out and hurried under the eaves of the warehouse to get out of the rain. The moisture penetrated Cadence's jacket and chilled her to the bone. She much preferred North Pole Kingdom snow; it landed on her clothes and wrapped her in magical warmth. She shivered and waited for Matt to unlock the door.

Once she entered, she couldn't hold back the exclamation. "Wow!" Joie spun around eyeing the stacks and stacks of boards and planks and sheetrock panels. "It's just like the one at North Pole Kingdom."

"Really?" Matt shrugged out of his jacket and hung it on a peg inside the door. "I'd have thought you'd have more electronic parts and such."

"Oh, we do." Joie smiled. "It's probably twenty times bigger than our lumber warehouse. We don't get as many requests for toys made out of wood. That's why ours is as small as yours."

"Small? You call this small?" Matt eyed her as if he didn't believe what she was saying. She'd just have to take him there one day. Maybe before her mission was finished they could take a tour of North Pole Kingdom. She'd love to show him the whole operation. It would put any construction company to shame. Even the biggest skyscrapers in the biggest cities were no match for the amount of materials that were part of Santa's workshops.

"You must be very proud of your company." Joie hadn't meant to undermine what he'd accomplished.

"It's taken me years to build this up." The pride shone through his voice. "I couldn't have done it without Cadence."

"She must have been a great support to you." Joie put that on the list of things to look for.

Matt nodded but didn't say anything.

Joie clasped her hands together and blew into them to warm them up. How could he take off his coat and not be cold? "What can I help you get?" She had to get moving or she'd be as frozen as a Popsicle.

He gestured for her to follow him. "I'll only need a few things. Just some sheetrock, tape, and mud."

She caught up to him. "Mud? You put mud on walls?"

Matt laughed, his deep voice booming through the space; the first time she'd ever heard him laugh. "It's called sheetrock mud. It's like plaster to fill in the cracks."

Joie couldn't help herself and giggled. She liked the sound of his laugh, so much deeper and resonating than the male elves, and completely different than Santa's boisterous one. Matt's was like dark chocolate with caramel and pecans. "I guess mud on a wall would be pretty silly."

He walked to a pile of small discarded pieces of sheetrock and picked one up and measured it. "Unless you lived in Mexico and called it stucco."

"Santa loves to deliver presents to the children there."

He handed her the sheetrock that was slightly bigger than the hole in the wall. "Why's that?"

She shifted the piece in her arms, the edges scratchy against her hands. "I think it's because they honor the birth of the Christ child. It's not so commercialized there."

Matt left the pile of sheetrock and moved to a storage room. "Really? How can anyone be sure there's a god who would send his son to this miserable place? Explain to me why there's so much suffering in the world."

Joie puzzled for a moment over his question. "Because this life is a test to see if we'll believe in Him, even when things are hard, and miserable, and unexplainable."

Matt didn't move or say anything for a moment. "Let's just get what we need."

Joie nodded. Another item to add to the list. Find someone who believed and would help Matt with his faith.

He took a small tub from a shelf and set it on the floor. "Mud." Then he grabbed a role of something that looked like giant cellophane tape only mesh-looking. "Drywall tape."

"Not only do you run a good company, you really know what you're doing." Joie loved working with wood. Could repairing a hole in the wall be so different?

"I've been doing this since I helped my dad build our house." He opened a drawer and pulled out a box of nails.

"Oh! I know what those are." She clapped her hands.

"Ah, you've used these before in Santa's workshop?" Matt picked up the items on the floor.

"I've built a few things in my life." Joie followed him out of the room.

"Like what?" Matt closed the door behind her and twisted the key in the lock.

"Trains and tracks mostly. A few doll houses." Joie couldn't help the excitement bubbling out. "But my most favorite of favorites was this special order dump truck. A little boy in Bosnia wanted it. Mrs. Claus gave the project to me."

Matt's eyebrows drew together. "Mrs. Claus? I thought the elves were run by Santa."

Joie shook her head. "That's what most people think, and Mrs. Claus kind of likes keeping it that way. Actually, Santa is in charge of deliveries and spying. You know the ones who bring back the information for the naughty and nice list."

"So Mrs. Clause pretty much runs the place."

Joie laughed out loud. "That's what Santa thinks, but really it's a joint operation. I guess it's kind of like marriage. They each have separate roles. They've been working together so well for hundreds of years."

Matt set his armload on the floor and retrieved his jacket. "How old is Santa?"

"Um, I think we celebrated his sixty-fourth birthday. He gets to retire next year, and his son and his wife are going to take over running North Pole Kingdom."

"Wait, you just said that they've been working together for hundreds of years."

Joie giggled. "Yeah, I guess I did." She smiled at his lack of understanding of how things worked at North Pole Kingdom. "The family business, as we lovingly call it, has been around since the first Kris Kringle started leaving toys and gifts for children."

"So it just gets passed down. What if one of the children didn't want the job?"

"Not want the job? Are you kidding? The sons practically fight over who gets to be the next Santa."

"Oh." He didn't sound convinced. But then this must all be pretty foreign to him, kind of like how she felt about her new form.

After Matt stashed the things in his hands in the back seat of the truck, he took the piece of sheetrock she still held and laid it on the floor.

Joie hadn't expected him to, but he opened the passenger door for her. The rain had stopped, but the ground was still soggy. Her foot slipped on the running board when she tried to climb into the truck. Matt grabbed for her to catch her as she fell backward, he missed, and she landed in the gravel. Sharp pain shot through her elbow and down her arm.

"Joie!" He bent and scooped her up and set her in the seat. "I'm so sorry."

"Sour patch kids, that hurts." She held out her arm. The fabric on the sleeve hadn't ripped and looked none the worse for wear, but dum-dums, that was painful. "Do you think it's broken?"

"Probably not. Pretty hard to break elbows. But we ought to put some ice on it." He attempted to push her sleeves back.

She pulled away from him. "Ouch, ouch, ouch...don't touch it."

"Let's take your jacket off so I can see it better." Matt took the collar and eased first her good arm out. "Is that too much?" he asked when he grabbed the other sleeves and pulled on it, slipping her hand free.

Joie took a sharp inhale at the pain, like a million needles jabbing her skin. "I'll be okay, I think."

Matt turned her arm over. "It's a little red." He kept his grip on her wrist.

Joie gasped. "Humans feel a lot of pain, don't they?"

"I suppose so."

His touch, while gentle, sent little shots up her arm. She couldn't tell if that was from her injury, or the feelings of something else.

"Let's get home and put some ice on it." He swiveled her legs into the car. Again, that odd sensation of electricity ran through where he touched her. She'd only injured her elbow, not her legs. Shuddering, she eased back into the seat.

“What’s wrong? Are you cold?” Matt draped her jacket over her shoulders, then took off his coat, and tucked it around her legs.

“A little, thank you.” His touch was making it hard to think.

He stood so close, she could feel the warmth of him as well as the heat through her leggings where his coat rested on her legs. “I probably should get some grips for the running boards. It’s just, that, well...” he paused. “I haven’t needed to before.”

“Didn’t your wife ever ride with you?”

“Yes, but she never slipped.”

Another item for the wife checklist – someone who was graceful, not clumsy, like Joie. Boy, the list just got longer and longer. She had no idea how she would managed to find the perfect woman for Matt.

CHAPTER TWENTY-SIX

Matt shivered and turned up the heater. Once more he'd given his coat away to something in distress. If he called her a woman, he might have to acknowledge the feelings he was beginning to feel for her. He had to keep reminding himself, she wasn't human but an elf. A dear little creature sent from the North Pole to fill a wish for Emily, and he just happened to be part of her fantasy.

He wasn't ready for another wife. How could he replace the woman who'd been perfect for him in every way? Yet, as he'd stood beside her, ministering to her injured elbow and then tucking his coat around her legs, his heart had raced at the nearness of her. His gaze had focused on her lips. Kissable, soft, he'd wanted to taste them. It was more than that drawing him in. Her persistence drove him crazy; her happiness was completely infectious, and her tender and gentle ministering to his daughter was inspiring. Taking a quick peek at her sitting beside him, he couldn't help but wonder what would happen to her once she'd accomplished her mission. She would disappear out of his life.

Wasn't that the plan?

Matt broke the silence. "Are you warm enough?"

"Yes, thank you."

"Good."

"Matt?"

"Hmm."

Joie paused for a long time and he wondered if the question she was about to ask was going to be awkward.

"What happened to the woman who was driving the other car?"

Matt gulped. He'd already faced so much with his wife's death and Emily's disability, he had no desire to add to his grief. "Six months in jail. And a four-thousand dollar fine. I didn't go to her court hearings or sentencing."

Joie put her hand on his forearm, wincing as she did. "Have you contacted her?"

"Why would I do that?" How could she even suggest such a thing?

Her words turned passionate. "Don't you think she's hurting, too? Not just from the accident and the jail time and the fines. I mean, can you imagine how she must feel, knowing that she killed someone?"

Matt clenched his jaw. His mother had suggested going to see Laura Milo. What would he say to her? "I forgive you for ruining my life? For tearing my wife from me and leaving my child crippled for the rest of her life?" His grip tightened on the steering wheel. He had to keep his words quiet for fear he'd start in on a tirade. "Her punishment will never bring my wife back."

"But don't you think – "

"I have thought. Long and hard. Every single night. Until my head feels like it's going to explode." He focused on the road in front of him, not wanting to talk about Laura Milo.

Joie removed her hand and folded them in her lap. "I'm sorry, Matt. I really am." Her voice came out quiet. She stared out the passenger window and didn't say anything until they reached his house. She didn't wait for him to open her door, but came around to his side, picked up the tape and nails and took them into the house.

Matt followed Joie into the house. Emily and her grandmother sat at the kitchen table with popcorn and cranberries. "What are you two gals up to?" Matt asked, trying to dispel the horrid clenching in his gut.

"We're making a garland for the Christmas tree." Emily held up her end of the strand she was working on.

Matt remembered stringing them with his mother when he was a kid. "I like them." Cadence found the activity tedious. She much preferred the store-bought pearl beaded ones. Every year she'd picked a different theme and went all out decorating the tree. At the end of each season, she'd store the box for a year and then donate the entire contents to various charitable places around the country – one year the children's home, another year the homeless shelter. The year before she died, she'd put the ornaments in separate packages, got the names of service men and women serving overseas. They'd sat unsent in the living room for weeks after Christmas was over. His mother finally came and disposed of them. He never asked what she'd done with them, but knowing his mother, she probably saved them until last Christmas and mailed them as Cadence would have done.

"I guess I better get started on that wall." He set the materials on the kitchen counter.

Joie stood quietly in the doorway. "Where do you want me to put these?"

He gestured. "On the floor right there is fine."

Joie stood next to Matthew, eyeing the damage she'd caused. "I'd like to learn how to repair that."

Mom looked up from threading a piece of popcorn. "Did you have a nice time?"

Matt glared at her. "Lovely." He didn't mean to be so curt with her. "Joie fell and hurt her elbow."

"Oh, dear." Mom left the table. "Let me look at that."

Joie held out her arm. "It doesn't hurt now as much as it first did."

"That's the funny thing with elbows." Mom chuckled. "Never did understand why they called it a funny bone. Anyway, nobody laughs when you bang it."

"I guess it's a human thing," Joie said.

Matt held his breath, waiting to hear his mother's response.

Mom chuckled. "Can you imagine a dog with a funny bone?"

Matt found himself chuckling in spite of himself.

"Do elves have funny bones?" Emily's question brought Mom roaring.

"Elves have lots of them, but they don't laugh when they bang them, either." Joie held her side. "It hurts to laugh, too."

"Okay, you three. Stop." Mom waved at them. "My side hurts, too."

Matt breathed a sigh of relief, glad that Joie had not mentioned the accident, the woman at fault, or finding a wife. He went into the utility room, took a razor knife and measuring tape from his tool belt, and returned to the kitchen. The ladies were still laughing and joking about elbows and funny bones.

Measuring the opening, he said over his shoulder, "As soon as we fix the hole, maybe we can all go get a Christmas tree." That would be a great distraction, and having Emily and his mother along would keep the conversation light, like it was now.

Mom waved her hand. "That wall can wait. Why don't you guys go get the tree right now, then we girls can decorate it while you fix the damage?" She smiled at Joie. "We haven't had family time in a long time."

"Can we, Dad?" Emily twisted around in her wheelchair.

"Why not?" Matt set the blade down and ruffled his daughter's hair.

Mom's mischievous smile spread across her face. "I think I'm going to stay right here and keep stringing cranberries and popcorn."

Was his mother trying to push them together? He wondered what would happen when she found out that Joie really was an elf. She'd change her tune pretty quick.

CHAPTER
TWENTY-SEVEN

When she stepped out of Matt's truck, the smell of pines hit Joie with such a force that she could have simply died of happiness right there and then. It also made her homesick. She missed the aromas of North Pole Kingdom, not only the trees, but the cinnamon from the snickerdoodles and vanilla dancing in the air from the cookie factory, the peppermint brewing in the candy cane factory. But most of all she loved the aroma of ginger from Mrs. Claus's kitchen. If only she'd gotten the chance to finish the ones she Emily were trying to bake.

Matt unfolded the wheelchair and nestled Emily into it and tucked a blanket around her legs. Joie let out an audible sigh. "I love how much love you put into taking care of Emily."

Emily looked up into her father's face. "He's the best dad, ever." She leaned forward and whispered, but loud enough for Matt to hear, "Except he's so cranky sometimes. I think it's because he doesn't have a grown-up lady to love him like Mommy did."

"Then we shall remedy that very soon."

"All right, ladies, stop plotting, will you?" Matt wheeled Emily through a row of pine trees.

Joie put her hand on Matt's to stop the chair, then took another deep inhalation of the delicious trees. "I could just die and go to heaven right now."

Matt looked down at her hand where it rested on his and then back at her face. "Do elves go to heaven when they die?"

"Of course they do." Joie removed her hand.

He nodded and with a broad sweeping hand he motioned to the mini forest they stood in. "Which one shall it be?"

"That one's so tall." Emily pointed to the one at the end of the path. "Can we get that one?"

Matt eyed the tree. "I'm afraid we'd have to cut a hole in the ceiling in order for it to fit."

Joie walked over to the pine tree and let her eyes follow the trunk to the top. This one was small compared to the ones they decorated in North Pole Kingdom. "It is awfully majestic in spite of how short it is."

"Short? That thing's got to be at least 20 feet." Matt put his hand on his hip and pulled his eyebrows together.

Joie snickered. "I thought everything's supposed to be bigger in Texas."

"'Cept mountains. We don't have any of those." Emily leaned forward as if it would give her better vantage of the massive Christmas tree.

"We are surrounded by them in North Pole Kingdom. It keeps uninvited guests out." She moved to another tree a bit shorter, but tall enough to accommodate the corner of the living room where the ceiling vaulted. From the upstairs balcony they could easily access the top of the tree so they could put either a star or an angel on top.

Matt pushed Emily and parked her next to the tree Joie was admiring. "It's got nice full branches. He turned it around. "No bare spots."

"Will the needles fall off?" Joie shook one of the limbs.

"This one, Daddy. I want this one." Emily touched the needles sending another whiff of pine into the already fragrant air.

"All righty, this is it." Matt lifted the tree as if it weighed nothing. He was certainly strong.

A young man appeared from behind a second row of trees. "Here, let me help you with that, sir. Where are you parked?"

Matt turned loose of the tree. "Blue truck over there. Thanks."

As the teen dragged it out, he called back over his shoulder, "You can pay the man over there. I'll tie this down for you."

Joie followed Matt and Emily to the front of the tree lot. A middle-aged man stood with a green apron, like the kind waiters wear, tied around his waist. He looked like an older version of the kid; he must be the father. "Do I know you?" Matt asked as he paid for the tree. "You look familiar."

The man studied Matt's face. "Don't think so." He finally shrugged, looking uncomfortable and asked, "Did you find the perfect one?"

"We did." Joie could hardly contain her excitement. Something strange floated in the air and she couldn't quite figure out why it didn't seem magical. She brushed it off like snow dust on a cold night. Nothing was going to shake her excitement.

Once they got home, she couldn't wait to get started decorating it. The problem with that was where to get ornaments. She hated to ask Matt to purchase them. She hated even worse to have to ask Wink for help. She was almost certain he was lurking somewhere nearby. Maybe that's why the sudden feeling of portends hung thick in the air.

"Wonderful," the man replied.

Joie left Matt's side and wandered back to the trees. She didn't look back at him because she didn't want him to suspect anything. When she could no longer see Matt, she whispered, louder than she probably needed to, "Wink. Wink."

He appeared next to her and took her hand. "What's up, Snickerdoodle?"

"I'm not your snickerdoodle." Joie pinched her lips together and jerked her hand free.

"You wouldn't call me just for anything." A smug smile thinned his lips.

"I need you to bring me a whole bunch of ornaments from Poinsettia Shop. Ask Millie to put them on my account and I'll settle up when I get back. Then go to Mistletoe Market and see if Kerri has any of those special garlands left, you know, the ones with the fairy lights in them. Oh, and I'll need – "

"What's in this for me?" he interrupted.

Oh, tootsie pops! He'd probably want some horrendous favor – like marriage. "I don't know...what you want?"

"You know what I want."

"Wink, I already told you I do not love you, and I'm not interested in any way."

"That's what you said." A dubious expression crossed his face. He wiggled his finger in a come here motion.

Joie bent down.

"If you really want to help Matt find a wife, then you'd better stop flirting with him." He looked up. "Oh, and by the way, here he comes. I'll tell you later the favor I want." And with that, Wink disappeared.

"Oh, hi, Matt. I was just uh..." Joie did not like lying, so she let the sentence drop.

"Talking to your friend...what was his name?"

"Wink, he um...he just stopped in to see me." Joie wrinkled her nose, she hated how factlets made her feel.

"Did you have a nice chat?" His question came off accusatory, like she was hiding something.

"Oh, jelly rings, he's going to do a favor for me." She put her hands on her hips. "Don't ask me any more questions about it. It's a surprise." She just couldn't let Matt know what she was up to.

"I hope this doesn't end in another disaster."

Joie didn't think Matt meant for her to hear.

"Oh, it won't. I promise."

They returned to the truck where the young man had finished

tying the tree down. Matt lifted Emily and put her in her seat. Joie put her hand on the handle and turned to look at the lot one more time, and that bit of homesickness hit her again.

Across the way, Miss Hall stood looking at a small tree, not quite as tall as the woman herself. She opened her wallet and thumbed through some money. Then shaking her head, she stepped to an even smaller one.

Joie's heart raced. Matt could be a hero and help her purchase a nice tree. She'd fall in love with him because he was such a wonderful man. Joie could head back to North Pole Kingdom. Her heart seized for a moment as if the north wind had wrapped his icy fingers around it. As homesick as she was, she hated the idea of leaving Matt. He might need her, and she wouldn't be here to help.

Matt's hand touched hers where it rested on the door handle pulling her out of her thoughts. "You going to get in or are you waiting for me to be the gentleman?"

Here was the perfect opportunity to finish her mission since she'd bumbled it with the tire incident. She yanked her hand out from under his, then grabbed him by the wrist. "Look, there's Miss Hall. She needs a tree and she doesn't have enough money. You should go pay for hers so that she can see how gallant you are." Joie tried to pull him away from the truck.

He captured her wrist, spun her around and with both hands on the frame of the truck, pinned her against the door, his hands pressing on her shoulders. "You have to stop this. Miss Hall just broken up with her fiancé and is probably not interested in me."

Joie's gazed lifted from Miss Hall to his face. The intensity of his blue eyes with their spark of fire in them made her breath catch and all of a sudden she couldn't breathe.

With his hands holding her and his body so close to her, her heart raced. Time stopped. Several emotions crossed his face. Joie put her hands on his chest, to push him away. Instead they stayed. His chest rose and fell under her fingers. Did his heart beat as fast as hers? She pressed her back into the truck.

Like a slow motion replay of the game Bubblegum Mischief, he lowered his lips until they touched hers. The warmth of them took her breath away. Pop rocks exploded in her stomach. As if they had a mind of their own, her hands slid up his chest, her fingers intertwining at the back of his neck. He stepped closer until his body touched hers, drawing her into a deeper kiss.

"Um, Dad..." Emily's confused voice came from the back seat. "Miss Hall is watching you."

Matt startled and stepped back, leaving Joie's heart still racing, and her palms sweating. He cleared his throat and turned to where Miss Hall was standing with the tiny tree next to her car.

Oh, Chick-O-Sticks! Joie was supposed to be helping him make a date with Miss Hall. A herd of angry reindeer chased the butterflies from her stomach.

CHAPTER
TWENTY-EIGHT

Matt casually sauntered over to Miss Hall, trying to pretend he'd never kissed Joie, except his heart still raced, and knots as big as Texas tied his stomach like a roped calf. Miss Hall was trying to hoist the tree onto the roof of her car. "Can I help you with that?"

Miss Hall dropped the tree. "That would be great."

"I'm sorry about your fiancé." Matt picked up the tree and set it on top of her car.

She held the top of the tree while Matt secured the bottom half through her window, shooting a quick glance at Matt's truck. Joie had gotten in and stared straight ahead. "Don't be. I decided that a long distance romance was just not going to work for us." Miss Hall smiled at him; nothing about it exhibited any happiness behind it. "I'm sorry to hear about the interruption of your date. I hope your house will be okay." The second part sounded sincere.

"Clara and I were not out on a date." How many times did he have to convince people that he had no interest in the nurse?

"Hmm...man, woman, cozy restaurant, nice meal. Looked like a date to me."

"Jealous?" Matt had no idea why that shot out of his mouth.

A burst of laughter flew out followed by a snort. "It looks like you already have a pretty serious relationship going on." She nodded towards Matt's truck. "You seem to get around a lot."

He ran his hand over the back of his neck. It felt like his first rodeo and he wanted to get off the bucking bronco right now before his butt hit the ground and the dust filled his mouth. "Look, Joie is just my friend."

"With benefits?"

"No! Of course not." Although, if Miss Hall hadn't come along, he had no idea just how long he might have kissed Joie. She had most decidedly stirred up feelings that surprised him. Matt pinched his lips together. He couldn't even explain what had happened to himself, so how was he going to justify his actions to Miss Hall?

He took a deep breath and smiled sheepishly at her. He had to admit, Miss Hall was attractive, and she liked kids. He really ought to consider her as a mother for Emily. Joie had pushed them together with that flat tire. Never mind that Miss Hall had nearly gotten him killed by running into him.

Miss Hall interrupted his thoughts. "You don't owe me any explanation. Who you date or who you take out to dinner is none of my business." She held out her hand. "Thank you for tying my tree to my roof."

"Miss Hall, why don't you let me follow you home, and then I can help you get it into your house."

"Call me Dawnetta." She almost looked like she was considering it. "I don't know. My mama will probably be sleeping. I can leave it on the car overnight."

"Let me at least take it to your door?" He had to get that kiss off his mind.

"Won't your *friend* be jealous?"

"Funny thing about Joie...she's trying to help me find a..." he couldn't say wife. That would scare her off for sure, especially since she'd just broken up with her fiancé. The last thing Matt wanted to be was a rebound.

"Another friend?" Dawnetta raised her eyebrows and glared at him.

"Yes, I mean, no." He clenched one fist, stuffed his other hand in his pocket and shifted his weight. "Ah, heck. Never mind." He turned and headed back to his truck. Dawnetta would never go out with him now, not after she saw him kissing Joie. If only that elf had left his love life in his own hands. Then again, if she hadn't showed up, he'd still be lonely and miserable. She opened up the possibility of falling in love again. Cadence would want him to move on, wouldn't she?

"Wait." Dawnetta sprinted up behind him. "I think I will take you up on that offer to help me with my tree."

"Really?" He smiled at her. "It's a date."

She flitted her eyes again to Matt's truck. "Well, let's not quite call it that."

Matt busted out laughing. Another not-date. He wondered what Emily and Joie would think. "Let me take my tree home first, and then I'll meet you at your place and help you get it set up."

"Why don't you bring Emily and your friend?"

She'd suggest that after watching Matt and Joie kissing? That's not a normal woman thing to do.

CHAPTER TWENTY-NINE

A million emotions raced through Joie. Being a human was exhausting. No wonder they needed so much sleep.

Emily huffed from the back seat. "I really like Miss Hall, and she saw Daddy kissing you. Now she'll never go out with him."

Joie turned in her seat, guilt stabbing at her. "Oh, sweetie. I'm so sorry. I don't know how that happened." She'd been sent to find a mother, not flirt with her client, as Wink suggested. Now Emily wouldn't get a mom, and she'd fail her mission.

"What are you going to do now? There aren't any more unmarried ladies in Miracle that want me." The tears hung thick in her voice.

"I don't know." Joie had sure messed things up since coming here. Maybe Matt would have found the right woman without her assistance. She had to push that kiss out of her mind. More than likely the feelings she was having were what every human felt in her position. Sure, in North Pole Kingdom, they had love, even though she'd never actually felt that kind of affection for someone of the opposite gender. This whole human thing was messing with her psyche.

Matt climbed into the truck, started the engine, and didn't say a word. A scowl creased his forehead.

Emily let out an audible huff. "Did Miss Hall like you helping her with her tree?"

"I have another not-date."

"With Miss Hall, really?" Emily asked from the back seat.

"That's wonderful." Although Joie's mouth said the words, her heart rebelled, sending little ice crystals through it.

Matt chuckled, but it sounded forced. "She wants us all to come."

"Even Joie?" Emily asked.

Joie swallowed the snow cone forming in her gut. "She really said that?"

"Awkward, huh?" Matt looked over at Joie and then back at the road.

She just couldn't go on a not-date with Matt. Maybe if she'd remained an elf, she could have lurked invisible, finding ways for them to get close. A little nudge here, a gentle push there and they'd be in each other's arms in no time, and their not-date would quickly morph into a date. As an elf, she wouldn't feel like she'd swallowed ribbon candy without chewing them first.

When they arrived at Matt's home, Joie unbuckled Emily, set her in the wheelchair, and pushed her toward the house, while Matt untied the tree and dragged it up the sidewalk, leaving pine needles in his wake.

Mom had left the strands of popcorn and cranberries lying in neat rows across the coffee table, ready to be hung on the tree.

Matt put the tree into the container the lot owner had given him and went to the kitchen.

Joie parked Emily next to the coffee table. "I don't think I should go to Miss Hall's house. I'm afraid I'll just mess things up." That was mostly truth with a little factlet thrown in. The real truth was that she didn't really want to see Matt falling for Miss Hall. Her stomach turned and turned like someone was making cotton candy in it. If this was how humans felt love, then she had to admit she had more than just misunderstood feelings for Matthew Adams. She was falling in love with him. She couldn't be. Mrs. Claus would surely demote her and send her off to work in the coal mine for not completing her mission.

"But I want you to come." Emily pouted. "Dad might need your help."

"I'm sure he'll do just fine without me." Joie sat on the couch and fingered one of the strands of popcorn.

Matt brought a pitcher of water into the room and poured it into the base. "Who will do fine?"

Joie rubbed her temples. "I'm getting a headache. Is it all right if I don't go with you? And if you want, I can keep Emily here with me. I promise, no baking cookies. I'll lay right here on the couch and Emily and I will watch movies."

"I want to go with you, Daddy." Emily pushed her chair toward her father.

"All right, pumpkin." He zipped up her jacket and pushed her toward the door. "I'll be back in a bit, and we can figure out how to get you home. Perhaps Wink can help you."

Joie fidgeted with the candy cane charm on her bracelet. "Maybe Miss Hall will let you help her decorate her tree. Go; have a fun time."

Matt gave her one last glance as he walked out the door. Why did she feel like her whole world had gone with him? Human love stunk like oranges left in the bottom of a Christmas stocking to rot.

After the sound of his truck faded into the distance, Wink popped in with mounds of boxes in all different sizes, each bearing the label of the store she'd requested. "Heya, girl. Why are you lying on the couch? We have work to do."

On any other given Christmas, she'd have popped up and sprung into action. "You do it." She pictured Matt and Miss Hall hanging ornaments together, popping corn, sipping hot cocoa, while she was stuck with Wink. His magic could have it finished in no time.

"Candy Buttons, this was your idea." His voice lilted as he tipped his head to one side and he punched his fists on his hips.

"Don't call me that." Joie sat up. "I hated it when we were kids. I especially hate it now."

Wink opened the first box and started unwrapping delicate ornaments surrounded in tissue and setting them next to the garlands Flora and Emily had made. With every ounce of will power, she picked up the first strand and hung it, draping it carefully on the branches.

Then the next and the next. After she had them all in place, she started in on the ornaments. By the time they'd emptied all the boxes, they'd transformed the room into a magical wonderland, one Mrs. Claus would be proud of. The floor-to-ceiling window framed the tree like an art piece in a gallery. From the balcony, Wink placed a silver and pink filigree star on top of the tree.

"That's not the one I ordered." Joie tapped her chin. "It doesn't even match."

A bit of mischief glinted in Wink's eye. "I have a secret about this particular one. You just trust me on this. Matthew is going to love it. But don't tell him that I put it there. I want it to be your idea. Believe me, he'll thank you for it."

For the final touch, she hung a swag of mistletoe from the balcony, placed right where a anyone coming in or out of the kitchen might get caught under it. She touched her lips, the taste of him no longer lingered there. She wished it did.

CHAPTER THIRTY

Matt and Emily stood outside Dawnetta's door. The paint was peeling, the roof over the porch sagged. Someone needed to fix that before it caved in. He raised his fist to knock and lowered it again. What was he thinking? Joie had pushed him into this, this finding a wife thing. First Clara, the nurse, and now the fifth grade teacher.

"Miss Hall is really nice." Emily said. "I think she'd make a good mommy."

That was the final push he needed. Joie had been right all along about his daughter needing a mother, especially since the accident left Emily disabled. Emily really liked Miss Hall. She could make his daughter happy, give her the attention that a girl growing up needed. He could date her and see where it led. If he should be feeling happy about moving forward with his life, why did his tongue turn to sandpaper and his throat feel like the Sahara desert?

"Aren't you going to knock?" Emily asked. "It's cold out here."

"Oh, right." Matt knocked.

Dawnetta answered the door. "Come on in." She'd changed her clothes and put makeup on. She hadn't needed to, she was pretty enough as it was.

Mrs. Hall sat on the couch going through a plastic bin, unwrapping ornaments, homemade from the looks of them.

"Mama, you remember Matt."

"Yes, I do." Mrs. Hall smiled up at him. "Thank you so much for rescuing my daughter again."

"It was nothing. The guy at the lot could have done the same thing." Matt pushed his daughter to the center of the quaint living room. The furniture was worn. The doilies on the arms of the sofa didn't do a very good job hiding the bare spots. It must be difficult living on a teacher's salary.

"But you did it, and that was awfully nice." Mrs. Hall set another ornament on the table.

Matt eyed the room trying to figure out the best place to put the tree. "Where would you like me to set it up?"

Dawnetta glanced from one corner to the next. "We usually put it there." She pointed to a rocker. "Since Mama got here, we had to make room for some of her things." The flush in her face looked even brighter against her blond hair. He had no idea what she had to be embarrassed about. While her home wasn't as big as his, and the furniture not as new, it was a roof over her head and looked like she managed just fine.

"I know." Emily held a half-unwrapped ornament on her lap. "You can push the piano over and move the rocker next to the piano. Push the couch into the corner where the rocker was. Then put the tree on top of the coffee table in front of the window so people will think you have a great big tree."

Dawnetta patted the top of Emily's head. "You are one smart little girl. I can't wait until you're in fifth grade.

Another reason to like Miss Hall. "Let's get it done." He pressed his back against the upright grand piano and pushed. It was heavier than he thought and didn't slide well on the carpet. A ripping of fibers sounded as he slid the antique into place. His heart sank.

"Oh, no. My carpet." Dawnetta rushed across the tiny room.

"I'm so sorry about that." Matt checked around the floor to see where he'd caused the damage. It must have been under the edge against the wall. "I can come back after Christmas and repair it when you take the tree down."

Tears had formed at the corners of her eyes and she brushed them away. "I've been wanting to replace it, but I just haven't had the funds. I'd hoped it would hold up until the summer." She shrugged her shoulders.

Matt wanted to offer to replace the whole room. Would she accept his gift? "Let me see what I can do. I have connections in my business."

"You'd do that for me?" Her eyes glistened with moisture that she kept trying to brush away.

"I broke it, I'll fix it."

Mrs. Hall kept darting glances between Matt and Dawnetta, a hopeful expression on her face.

Matt rubbed his hand along the back of his neck. "Let's get the rest of the furniture moved."

Once they had the tree placed in front of the window, Mrs. Hall sat in the old rocker, pulled her smart phone out, and put on some Christmas music. She smiled all the while the three of them hung blue tinseled garlands, silver strands of tinsel and handmade ornaments on the Christmas tree.

After he plugged in the lights, they stepped back and admired their handiwork.

"You did a good job, Daddy." Her face beamed up at him. "Almost as pretty as Mommy's."

Not bad, if he did say so himself. "I need to get this little one home and to bed."

Dawnetta looked at her cell phone. "Oh, my goodness, look at the time. I've kept you from decorating your own tree."

"It's all right. We can do it after church tomorrow. Huh, Daddy?"

"That's a good idea." Matt put Emily's coat on her. "I can't remember the last time I had so much fun decorating a tree. Cadence always took care of it." He looked at his boots and then back up at her, his heart stuck in his throat. He had to remember he was doing this for Emily. "Can I ask you out on a date?"

She handed him his coat. "I'd like that, but what about your friend?"

CHAPTER THIRTY-ONE

Joie stood in the middle of the living room admiring her finished touches. Even though she loved how it turned out, she hoped Matt wouldn't be disappointed that she didn't wait for him. It would have been fun to decorate it all together, but then, Joie liked doing things herself, and she loved the element of surprise she knew would happen when Matt and Emily walked in to find the room all dressed up as it was.

The twinkling lights on the tree accented the red and gold ornaments and the strands of popcorn and cranberries. Pine garlands tied with candy-cane-striped bows hung along the banister, matching the bows on the tree and the fabric covers on the furniture. Everything about the front room spoke of a North Pole Kingdom Christmas.

Decorating the living room was just a start. She couldn't wait to add holiday touches to all the rooms. The next room she'd tackle would be the kitchen. But first Matt needed to complete the repairs on the wall.

Wink crossed his arms and leaned against the grandfather clock. "We make a pretty good team."

Joie rolled her eyes. Technically, it was all her ideas and know-how that made the whole thing come together. If she still had her magic, she could have decorated without Wink's assistance. It was nice that he was willing to aid her after she'd rejected him. "Thanks for all your help this evening. I think Matt will be surprised."

"So you still have a sweet tooth for that guy, huh?"

Joie shook her head. She didn't dare tell Wink how she really felt about him. "I just told you that because...well, I'm not interested in you, and he just happened to be there...and..." her words trailed off. Was there a time when telling a lie felt right? Or a time that telling the truth felt so wrong? This being-a-human thing sure had her confused.

The headlights of Matt's truck pulling into the driveway shined through the big picture window.

"That's my exit cue." Wink disappeared.

Joie did one last circle of the living room, making sure everything was exactly as it should be. She smiled at her handiwork, glad Wink had insisted on helping her. She guessed he wasn't such a pest after all.

With hands clasped in front of her, she waited for Matt and Emily to enter. She held her breath, hoping they loved the decorations.

Matt pushed Emily through the door and stopped short. Emily gasped. "It looks like a fairy land."

"Do you like it?" Joie waited for Matt's reply.

He stayed silent for so long studying the room that she feared his disapproval. He finally spoke. "You got it just right."

"She got Miss Hall right, too. Huh, Daddy?"

Matt's face colored. "Maybe she did." His eyes studied Joie's for a moment.

Her heart sank. He must have had a nice time tonight with Miss Hall. Which meant the kiss between them had meant nothing. "I'm glad I could help." She forced her words to sound bright. "Did you ask her on a date?"

"As a matter of fact, I did." He didn't sound so happy about it.

"Then, I guess I should head back to North Pole Kingdom." Joie fingered the candy cane charm on her bracelet as if she was ready to go back home, but she didn't want to go. While she was homesick, all she wanted to do was stay here with Matt. Her heart ached. Never before had Joie felt so conflicted.

"Can't you stay a little longer? The church Christmas party is on Monday night." Emily looked so hopeful. "I get to be an angel in the nativity."

"There's a potluck as well. I'm sure you could help us make a tasty dish. Maybe some of those gingerbread cookies you started to make yesterday?"

"Are you considering going to church after all you'd professed about your disillusionment about God?" Had Miss Hall helped him overcome his disbelief? If so, then perhaps she was the right woman after all.

"I have to go see my daughter in the play." His voice came out bitter.

"You don't go to church, I take it," Joie asked.

"Not since Cadence died."

Watching his daughter in the nativity production was the only reason he was going. Joie shouldn't have been surprised. At least it was a start.

"Please, Joie, you have to stay so you can see me, too," Emily begged.

"All right. But where will I sleep?" Joie had already caused quite a stir among the neighbors which had reached Matt's mother.

Emily clasped her hands as if pleading. "She can sleep in my room with me."

Matt helped his daughter out of her coat. "She does have an extra pull-out bed."

"That would be lovely. Thank you." Joie frowned. "What will the neighbors think when they see that I'm staying here?"

Matt laid Emily's coat across her lap. "We'll just tell them I hired a nanny to take care of her."

"But that's not the truth." Now that she was in a human body, Joie didn't like how she felt, even when she told a factlet.

"It's much more believable than telling them you're an elf from the North Pole." Matt took his jacket off and hung it over the handles on the wheelchair. "Besides, you are tending Emily, or at least you will be while I attempt to find a wife."

"But I'm supposed to help you do that." Joie hated the idea of her not being with Matt to be his aide.

Matt gave a short huff. "By babysitting Emily, it allows me free time to pursue looking for a wife."

A wife. Joie rubbed her palms together. "What about your mother babysitting? She even said she would."

Matt swallowed as if he had a lump caught in his throat. "Since you're stuck as a human, I can't have you trailing me. You know what happened when Dawnetta saw us together."

Kissing. Joie hadn't meant – that was all Matt's doing. "But it didn't turn out so bad. You now have a date with her."

"Right." Matt shifted his weight. "Since you're going to be *staying* here...I might as well put you to work to earn your room and board." He headed toward the stairs, then turned back to Joie. "By the way, the living room looks lovely." Before he started up the stairs, he added, "If you'll get Emily ready for bed, I'll change my clothes and work on repairing the kitchen wall."

Matt climbed the stairs to the balcony. He stopped to look over the railing at the decorations. "Cadence would have approved." He moved to the master bedroom at the end of the balcony. The click of the door behind him echoed a pang in her chest. She touched her lips trying to conjure the feeling of the kiss. It had dissipated like steam from a cup of hot chocolate.

Emily yawned. "We helped Miss Hall decorate her tree. We moved her furniture and everything." She rubbed her eyes and sighed. "I think Miss Hall is even better than Ms. Evans."

A growing knot tightened her stomach. Joie gripped the handles of Emily's wheelchair, Matt's thick jacket warm under her touch. She wheeled Emily down the hall to her room. Once inside, Joie picked up the jacket and brought it to her nose. It smelled delicious, like spice drops and something else, not like any of the flavors from North Pole Kingdom. Definitely Matthew Adams. She held it to her face, luxuriating in the scent and the warmth, imagining his kiss again. Her tummy tingled.

Zagnuts! Why did she have to go and fall for a human? Why couldn't she have been content with an elf, someone more like her? She shook her head and dropped his jacket on Emily's desk.

"I'm not tired." Emily interrupted her thoughts. "Can we play a game?"

"One game of Twinkle Brite and then off to bed with you." Joie took Emily's coat off her lap and hung it in the closet. "First, tell me where your pajamas are."

CHAPTER THIRTY-TWO

Matt plopped on the edge of his bed. Why had he asked Joie to stay? He'd already made up his mind about Miss Hall, never mind that he hardly knew her. That moment he kissed Joie played over and over. She'd drawn him to her like a sailor to a siren. The way her mouth responded to his, he knew she wanted him to kiss her.

He tried to picture that same kiss with Dawnetta. Every time he imagined it, Joie's lips thrust into his memory. Not just her lips, but her eyes, her skin, her slender form. Mostly it was her kindness and happiness. He'd never met anyone as bubbly and happy all the time.

If she'd just been a real human to begin with, things might have turned out differently between them. He couldn't fall in love with an elf. It would never work. He shook his head, trying to rid the feelings piercing his heart. Once she went back to her elf form, her feelings for him would change. She'd lose those human feelings and desires and go back wanting a relationship with someone like her...Wink, maybe.

Matt took his shirt off and threw it in the hamper. Digging through his drawer, he found a grungy t-shirt perfect for working on the damaged wall. He pulled it over his head and went into the bathroom to comb his messed up hair, not that he cared what Joie thought of his looks.

The reflection of his silk-screened shirt blared back at him. "Fight for Love," it read with a pair of boxing gloves dangling from the O. He couldn't wear that one, especially around Joie.

He hurried back to his dresser, peeled off the offending piece of clothing, threw it in the trash, and found a plain gray shirt.

Once he went downstairs and into the kitchen, he used his razor knife to even out the edges where the firemen had hacked through the sheetrock, cutting it wide enough to expose two studs to attach the new piece. Next, he took out his measuring tape and measured the wall, then cut a piece from the sheetrock, and began the process of fitting the sheetrock to the hole, making sure he knew where the studs were so he'd have something to hammer the sheetrock into, to hold it in place.

The doors swished when Joie entered the kitchen. "Emily is asleep."

"That was fast." Matt set the panel in place and hammered a nail into the sheetrock. "She never goes down this early. It's usually a battle every single night, even when she's exhausted and tells me she isn't tired, and I know better." Even Cadence could never get her to bed on time.

"I played a game with her and then sang her my mother's favorite song."

"Did she brush her teeth? Read her a story?"

Joie pulled her eyebrows together as if trying to remember. "Uh, yes and yes, and I helped her say her prayers."

"I think perhaps we should call you, Saint Joie."

She giggled. "Hardly."

He hammered in a couple of nails. "Hand me that role of tape."

Her hand brushed his when she placed it next to him on the counter. She jerked back as if he'd burned her.

"I suppose the decorations you did tonight remind you of the North Pole." Matt took the tape, cut off a section and placed it over the spot needing to be seamed.

"They do." A slight smile crossed her lips and then vanished. "Wink helped me."

He opened the tub of spackling and gave it a thorough stir. "So you and Wink made up."

Joie shook her head. "Oh, no, I mean, yes, we're friends again. He understands that we're just not meant to be." Sadness clouded her eyes that were normally so bright and lively.

He cleared his throat. "That's good."

She drew her eyebrows together in a puzzled expression. "Why is that good? Don't you want to see me happily married as well?" Her voice came out a bit snippy.

Matt didn't know why he said that. "Of course, you deserve to find love. We all do." His cell phone rang interrupting their conversation.

"Hey, Matt. Long time, no talk." Ethan's voice sounded like he was talking from the bottom of a well.

"What's up?"

"Look, I have a huge favor to ask you. I'm coming home for Christmas, but it's a surprise, so I don't want anyone to know I'm here. Is there any way you could put me up for a few days?"

Matt looked at Joie and had no idea how to explain her to his friend. "My house is kind of full right now. I already have a guest. Can you stay at my mom's?"

"Perfect." The phone crackled with static.

"There's a church Christmas party and I'm pretty sure your family will be there. What a great way to surprise them." Matt hoped Ethan managed to catch all that before the line went dead.

"I suppose I could stay with your mother." Joie did not look like that's what she wanted to do.

He turned back to Joie. "You're already here. And besides my mother adores Ethan. We were best friends in high school. He spent a lot of nights at my house when his parents went out of town."

"You're sure?"

"Positive." Matt patted her hand. "I guess I should get back to work."

An awkward silence filled the kitchen. Finally, Joie pulled up a chair and knelt on it, leaning over the counter, her face close to where Matt pressed the mesh tape along the seams. "Can I help you?"

"Sure." Matt handed her a strip of the tape. "You hold one end against the seam." He held her hand as she placed the tape against the piece of sheetrock and wall. The smoothness of her skin and smallness of her fingers in his sent a bit of spark up his arm. He didn't turn loose of her hand when she'd drawn the strip along the seam. "You do that really well."

She hadn't twisted her fingers from his. "Thanks – not much different than doll houses."

Reluctantly, he turned loose of her hand so he could give the spackling another stir. "You'd be really good working in my company doing the final touches on the buildings and homes we erect." He handed her the spatula. "Want to give it a try?"

Joie dipped a glob onto it and ran it over the tape, pressing it into the mesh and the crevice. "It's kind of like frosting a cake." She kept scooping spackling from the tub until she'd gone all the way around the square piece, then handed him back the spatula.

"You did great." Matt dabbed at a few of the spots sticking up.

"Okay, now what?" she asked.

"Now we wait." Matt snapped the lid back onto the tub.

"For what?" Joie climbed off the chair.

He took the spatula to the sink and ran water over. "For the mud to dry, then we texture it and let it dry. After that we can paint."

"I love painting." For a moment the twinkle came back into her eyes. He liked when she got excited about something. "You should have seen the doll house I decorated. It had stairs and wall paper, that wasn't really wall paper. I painted all the tiny flowers. Each room had a different design. Mrs. Claus said it was the prettiest doll house she'd ever seen." She gave a soft sigh, pulled out the chair and sat, resting her chin in her hand. A faraway look drifted across her face.

"You must be really missing the North Pole." He should probably tell her that he planned on seriously dating Dawnetta Hall. But not yet. He didn't want her to leave.

"A little." She avoided his eyes and drew little circles on the table with her finger.

Again that awkward silence crept between them. Talking to her had been so much easier before she'd become a human. It was like an electric current ran between them and he didn't dare speak for fear of electrocuting her. Matt cleared his throat. "Are you hungry?"

"No, Wink brought me a slice of ham and some sweet potatoes."

"Ah." Matt shook the water off the spatula and dried it with a paper towel.

Joie put her hand over her stomach, pressing it flat. "How did your not-date with Miss Hall go?"

"I helped her put her tree up." He knew what question was coming next. He didn't know how to explain to her about Dawnetta.

"Did it look nice?" She still kept her eyes on the floor.

"Not as pretty as the one you did, but it was homey, nice." The corners of his mouth tugged into a small smile. "A lot of the ornaments were old and some of them homemade, and a couple of them were pictures Mrs. Hall's children had made at school."

"Those are sweet. We do that at North Pole Kingdom as well." She looked up at Matt, her eyes shining with moisture.

"Look, you don't have to stay until the Christmas party if you don't want." He sat in a chair next to her. He wanted to take her hand in his. If only she hadn't been an elf.

The look of sorrow in her eyes sent a prickle to his heart. "You want me gone?" she asked.

"Oh, no, that's not what I meant." The thought of her leaving turned his stomach inside out. Now that she couldn't pop in and out on him, he liked having her around. He realized she was an amazing, gifted woman. He meant elf; she was a gifted *elf.*

CHAPTER

THIRTY-THREE

Joie sat on the trundle bed Matt had pulled out from under Emily's bed. He still hadn't told Joie what happened while he was at Miss Hall's house. She shouldn't be jealous. After all, if the two found common interests and fell in love, it was the perfect solution to Emily's request. Dawnetta loved children and seemed to really like Emily.

Joie's heart ached. She didn't want him to fall for Dawnetta. She wanted him to love her. He'd never see her as anything other than an elf.

She touched her lips. He had kissed her. Had that meant anything to him? It didn't seem like it. The next moment he'd run off to be with Miss Hall. Wasn't Joie supposed to find a wife for Matt? A mother for Emily?

Joie decided she hated being a human. As an elf, there was never these kinds of horrible, mixed up emotions. Elves found mutual compatibility, got married and had lots of little elves. The odd thing about being an elf, is Joie had never found another elf she had any interest in. Now that she thought about it, she'd even wondered if she belonged in North Pole Kingdom. What would Mrs. Claus think if she never went back? Would her adult humanness take away the magic of Christmas? Would she become like the rest of humanity and only pretend to believe in Santa Claus to keep the children happy?

Joie curled her knees up to her chest and rested her forehead on her arms where they wrapped around her legs. What was Mrs. Claus thinking, sending an inexperienced elf on such an important assignment?

Wink popped in and sat in the chair across from the bed. "You look all black licorice sticks and sour patch kids."

The last person Joie wanted to see was Wink. She looked up at him. "What are you doing here?"

"I was worried about you." His feet almost reached the floor, but not quite. He swung them as if he was peddling an imaginary bike in the air.

"I'm fine."

"You still insisting on staying here?"

"Until I know that Matt has found a wife." Frustrated, she clenched her pajama bottoms. Well actually they belonged to Cadence. She did not need him rubbing her situation in her face.

"It looks like he may have just done so." Wink grinned and raised his eyebrows.

Joie stood and paced the room. "Miss Hall, I know."

Wink followed her with his gaze. "Miss Hall thinks he's pretty wonderful. So congratulations."

"I don't want your congratulations." Joie slumped back onto the bed, bent over and tried not to cry.

"Oh, I get it." Wink crossed the room and patted her back. "You really have fallen for him, haven't you? That whole business in the hotel about pretending to be in love with him was to throw me off... deep down you must have really meant it."

The tears prickled at her nose and threatened to break free. "I didn't realize it then." She choked back a sob. "I've really messed things up, haven't I?"

"Nah. Mrs. Claus and all the other elves will take you back. You'll get over him and in time, you'll find another...." He eyed her for a moment. "Maybe not an elf, if the Clauses can't turn you back."

"I can't stay in North Pole Kingdom like this." Joie straightened up and motioned to her body, her freakishly long arms and big feet. Sure she looked good as far as humans went, but she'd made such a mess of everything in this form. "Oh, Wink, what am I going to do?"

"You still have your candy cane charm, so you could just come home and forget this ever happened." Wink hopped onto the bed next to her. "Besides, it looks like Matthew is going to marry Miss Hall anyway. So see, all he needed was just a nudge in the right direction."

A giant stab of frosted icicles went through her heart. "I guess you're right."

"Come with me right now." Wink held out his hand.

Perhaps Wink was right. She should just leave now and try and sort everything out with Mrs. Claus. Joie wrapped her fingers around the charm and brought it to her lips.

From the darkness in the room, Emily's sleepy voice said, "But you promised to go to the Christmas party."

Joie dropped the candy cane. "I suppose I did." The party was in two days. She could stick it out that long, couldn't she?

Wink released her hand and hopped off the bed. "I'll see you in two days. Remember, you still owe me a favor." He disappeared as quick as letters to Santa on December twenty-fifth.

"I don't like Wink." Emily's voice sounded wide awake.

Joie's face flushed warm and she was glad Emily couldn't see it. "How much did you hear?"

"That you love my daddy." Emily propped up on an elbow, her silhouette small and fragile in the barest light coming from the night light.

Joie gulped. She didn't want to ask, but if, and that was a huge snowball *if*, Emily considered her as a possible mother. Joie had to know. "How does that make you feel?"

"Oh, lots of ladies like my dad. It's me that's the problem." She sounded more irritated than anything. "Miss Hall really likes my dad. I could tell when he was helping her with the tree. And I could tell that my dad really likes her, too."

"And she likes you, too." Joie finished, trying to hide the sadness in her voice. That was all she needed to hear. North Pole Kingdom was where Joie belonged. "She'll be a great mother for you."

"But you will stay for the Christmas party, right?"

"Yes, dear. I'll stay, and then I really have to return to North Pole Kingdom." Joie lay back onto her trundle bed and rolled over to face Emily. "You are the greatest kid ever. Miss Hall is one lucky woman to be the mommy to such an amazing little girl."

Joie stroked Emily's head until she fell asleep. It was going to be a very long two days. She hoped Matt would find things to do so she didn't have to be around him.

CHAPTER THIRTY-FOUR

Joie fastened Emily's seatbelt in the backseat of Flora's sedan. Once she got the girl settled she slipped into the front with Matthew's mother. "Thank you so much for letting me come along."

"We did this last year on the anniversary of Cadence's death. Matt never wants to come." Flora backed the car out of the driveway and headed toward Windfall, several miles from Miracle.

The long stretch of two-lane highway gave Joie plenty of opportunity to ask Matt's mother about him and to make sure Dawnetta Hall was really the right choice for a wife and mother.

"You know I could have watched Emily while he went out with that teacher." It also gave Flora the opportunity to question Joie.

"I owe Matt for nearly destroying his house. It's the least I can do to repay him for the damage." Butterfingers, she did not want to talk about herself. That would lead her to conjure all kinds of factlets.

"Why he's not dating you is beyond me."

"That's because Joie is an elf and she has to go back to the North Pole just as soon as Daddy finds me a new mommy." Leave it to an eight-year-old to tell the truth.

"About that." Flora smiled at her granddaughter through the

rearview mirror before turning to Joie. "I hardly know anything about you."

Here it went. She either told the truth and let Flora think she was a nougat-filled nut case, or lie and live with the guilt. Both options were horrible.

"She's really an elf." Emily's voice grew more insistent.

Flora laughed. "Now where would a child get that silly notion?"

Joie took a deep breath. "Because she's telling the truth?" Joie drew her eyebrows together and the corner of her mouth turned down.

"An elf?" Flora took her eyes off the road for a moment and glanced at Joie.

Joie closed her eyes, clenched the bottom of her t-shirt, the one she'd pulled from the last box of Cadence's clothes ready to be donated to a charity. "Did you ever question why I'm wearing Matt's wife's belongings? Why I don't seem to have a home?"

"You're wearing her clothes?" As if looking at Joie for the first time, she ran her gaze from the shirt to the jeans and down to the shoes and gasped. "You are in Cadence's clothes." She decelerated and stared openly at Joie.

Flora pulled down a lane and stopped the car. By the time Joie finished telling Flora the whole story, Emily's letter, the fire, the miracles, everything, all Matt's mother could do was stare open-mouthed. "What if I told you I don't believe in elves?" She turned hastily in her seat and glanced at Emily. "I mean, just for opposition's sake."

Joie touched her hair before pulling the locks behind her pointed ears. "They're real. It's the only thing I got to keep when I turned into a human. You can pull them if you want."

Flora didn't hesitate and gave them a slight tug. "You could have had them altered, plastic surgery or something."

"I could have, but I didn't." Joie knew the perfect way to prove she was an elf. "I'll bet I can tell you the perfect Christmas gift you wanted when you were a child?"

With a bright smile, Flora leaned her head back. "I don't know about that. It was pretty special."

"Hey, Wink?" Joie called out. "I need your help." Somehow she knew he was close by.

Just as she suspected, Wink appeared in the back seat, beside Emily. "Hey, Candy Buttons."

Flora jumped. It was a good thing they were parked or they might have ended up in a ditch.

Joie rolled her eyes. "I told you not to call me that."

"Who is that?" Flora hung her arm over the backseat and eyed Wink.

"This is my friend, Wink." Joie motioned to her friend. "He's from North Pole Kingdom and has been helping me."

Flora continued to eye Wink. "I...I...don't know what to say."

Wink got up on his knees and held out his hand. "Most people say, "hello" or "how do you do?"

Tentatively, Flora took his hand. "It's nice to meet you." She raised her eyebrows and looked Wink up and down.

Wink took her hand. "Likewise."

Flora held onto him, running her thumb over the back of his hand. "You feel real enough."

"Of course, I'm real." Wink withdrew his hand and turned to Joie. "Now, why did you call me?"

"Do you know who Flora's watching elf was when she was a little girl?"

"Hmm...not sure. I'll have to go back and check the records." Wink looked thoughtful. "I'll be right back." Before he disappeared, he glanced back at Flora. "Let me guess, you need to prove that we really do take the naughty and nice lists back to Santa and report about what the child asked for."

"Right as Tootsie Pops." Joie knew he was the right one to ask. "I need to know what special Christmas gift she received when she was..." She turned to Flora. "How old were you?"

Flora waved her hand. "I don't need any more proof."

"It's no trouble." He gave Flora a quick wink.

"Eight. I was Emily's age." For all Flora seeming convinced, it looked as though she needed one more little push.

"I'll be back in a wink." Wink chuckled at his joke and then vanished.

Again, Flora jumped. "My, such comings and goings. That's enough to convince anyone he's an elf." She gave Joie a steady stare. "You, on the other hand, why aren't you elf-like?"

"She turned into a human using one of the miracles on her bracelet." Emily spoke up.

"Is that so?" This time her eyes grew narrow. "If you're supposed to find a wife for my son, how does being a beautiful human help? It seems to me that you'd only distract him."

Yeah, that's what Joie had realized as well. "It was an accident. I hadn't meant to use up the miracles Mrs. Claus gave me to help find a wife. I have this one left, but I'm scared to use it."

"Let me guess; you now are stuck as a human and can't be of much help."

"Daddy kissed Joie, too." Emily piped up from the back seat.

"Really?"

Joie couldn't tell if Flora was irritated or...what was that look on her face? Joie gulped. "But it looks like Matt's preference is Dawnetta Hall. So my job is done here and I'll be heading back to North Pole Kingdom."

"Hmm...that's too bad." Flora seemed genuinely sad.

Wink appeared in the back seat. "It was a saddle, blanket, halter, and tack."

"Actually, that's what I asked Santa for, but not what I got."

Wink chuckled. "You're right. It was a beaded bracelet with horse charms on it. Silver."

A faint smile crossed Flora's face. "I wanted a horse, but since we couldn't afford it, I asked for the gear. My dad told me I was silly to want that without an animal to put it on. I had to settle for the bracelet."

"But you finally got a horse when you were older, huh?" Emily asked.

"Yes, I did." Flora turned to the backseat. "Well, I'm definitely convinced now. You really are an elf." She shook her head.

"Thanks, Wink." Joie hated the idea of being indebted to him.

"I'll just add it to the favors you're going to owe me when you get back to NPK." And then he winked out.

"NPK?" Flora asked.

"North Pole Kingdom."

"Oh," Flora said as if the reality of Joie being an elf had settled completely on her.

CHAPTER
THIRTY-FIVE

Joie sat in the front seat of Flora's car. Her insides couldn't make up their mind how they wanted to feel. Icicles one minute, sour belts the next. All she knew was that she was there to make a difference, to help the family find peace – and find a wife for Matt.

Once they reached the gates, Flora drove past the gatehouse and to the back of the cemetery. Passing several headstones, they finally parked under a huge magnolia tree. Emily picked up her bouquet of phlox and hothouse roses, sprinkled with baby's breath and ivy. "Mama's favorites," Emily had explained when they'd stopped at the florist's shop.

"She'll love them." Joie loved the fragrance drifting through the car.

Flora pointed to where a woman in a dark coat with a hood up over her head knelt beside Cadence's headstone. "I wonder who that is."

Joie followed Flora's gaze. The woman appeared to be weeping. "Another relative?"

Flora shook her head. "No, not the right height or shape of any of Cadence's relatives."

"Maybe it's the lady who killed mama." Emily lifted her body so she could see over the dash board.

A slight, misty drizzle covered the windshield making it hard for Joie to see.

"I guess we should find out." Flora opened her door and left the warmth of the car. "You stay here, and I'll be right back."

Unsure whether Flora could manage without someone to perhaps mediate, Joie left the car and followed Flora across the soggy grass, the moisture penetrated the tennis shoes she'd borrowed from Cadence's wardrobe and soaked her socks.

Upon hearing their approach the woman leaned on a cane and struggled to stand. Her gaze flitted between the two women.

"Laura Milo?" Flora asked.

The poor woman looked as if she'd been caught stealing sugar plums from Santa's stockings. "Yes." Her voice came out weak, scared even.

Joie felt caught between the two woman, unsure what might happen. There needed to be some amends. Before either woman could speak, Joie wrapped her arms around Laura. "This has been a horrible two years for you, as it has been for Cadence's family."

Laura nodded; the tears streamed down her face. "I'm so sorry."

Flora worked her jaw as if holding back angry words.

Joie took Flora's hand then Laura's. "It's forgiveness and love that heals. You can say you're sorry for the rest of your life, and it will never change what happened."

Neither of them spoke. Joie continued. "Hearts can mend and the sorrowful can find peace."

Laura released Joie's hand, switched her cane and then took Flora's hand. "I've written to your family so many times, but the words felt lame. I know they can never bring your daughter back or heal that little girl. Please, forgive me."

A presence wrapped around them, softening their expressions. Flora's eyes glistened as she dropped Laura's hand and wrapped her in an embrace.

Joie smiled. Here was a miracle she hadn't even needed to use. If only Matt could have been here, he'd have felt it as well.

Flora released Laura. "Emily is with us. Would you like to meet her?"

"I'd love that."

Flora went back to the car to retrieve Emily.

"Are you Cadence's sister?" Laura asked.

"No, I'm just a good friend of the family." Joie hoped she didn't need to explain any further.

Laura nodded, wiping at the tears streaking her face. "How's Mr. Adams doing?"

"Better."

"I hope you have a good Christmas."

Joie could sense the genuine feeling behind Laura's words. "Christmas is always better with family."

Flora pushed Emily to the grave. For the moment, Emily ignored Laura. Maybe the little girl didn't want to meet the woman who'd left her paralyzed.

"Mrs. Milo is here today, Mama." Emily's words surprised Joie. "I think it's a good thing 'cuz she needs to feel better, too." She picked one of the phloxes from the bouquet and laid the rest of the flowers in the grass beside the headstone. "I miss you. But Joie, that's my friend right here." She held out her hand for Joie to take. "She's helping Daddy find a new mommy for me. I hope you don't mind. And Grandma came with us. And this lady here...she's the lady who didn't know she was making a bad choice. I know she feels real bad or else she wouldn't be here. I hope you're happy where you are. I love you, Mama." She started to sit up, but slunk back down. "And I'll try to be real good for my new mommy. I hope you don't mind that daddy is getting me a new mommy."

She handed the bunch of phlox to Laura. "I think mommy wants you to have this. I'm Emily."

"Thank you, Emily."

Emily pointed to the cane. "You're crippled, too."

Laura nodded.

"Do people love you anyway?"

Laura pulled her eyebrows together. "My husband and sons still love me."

"That's good." Emily rested her elbow and put her chin on her fist. Joie recognized the thoughtful gesture, the wheels in her brain turning at an idea. Her head popped up. "I know! You and your family should come to our church Christmas party tomorrow night."

Flora, who'd remained quiet through the exchange, smiled. "Yes, that would be wonderful. I'm sure Matt could use the opportunity to chat with you."

"Are you sure he'd want to see me?" Concern crossed Laura's face.

"Of course he would," Emily said.

Seeing Laura and forgiving her, Matt could not only move on, but find happiness as well. Then not only could Joie return to North Pole Kingdom with her mission accomplished, but she'd show Mrs. Claus the added bonus of bringing healing to both Matt's and Laura's hearts.

CHAPTER THIRTY-SIX

Matt shook the rain off his umbrella and paused before he entered the house. His feet ached, his head ached. His heart heavy. His date with Dawnetta had gone well enough. She had a lot of love in her heart. He could tell by the way she treated her mother; the kids at the school seemed to really like her.

Why couldn't he shake the feeling something was missing? Like the sparkle in her voice when she talked, the bounce in her step, the joy radiating from her face? Why was he comparing Dawnetta to Joie? He should be making the comparison to his deceased wife.

Matt held onto the door handle longer than he meant, staring at the blue paint. Prussian blue to be exact. Cadence had wanted the shade of the door to accent perfectly with the lighter colored shutters. Everything Cadence did had to be exact, right down to the Christmas decoration.

He opened the door and stepped into the heavenly aroma of ginger, vanilla, and warm sugar – and no kitchen fire. The lit tree graced the front window, lit garlands strung from the banister and railing on the balcony above accented the perfect décor. Matt followed the tree to where a familiar star graced the top-most bough.

Matt had to choke down the lump growing in his throat. He and Cadence had picked it out their first year of marriage. It had adorned their tree every year until the year she died.

Maybe Joie hadn't known that placing that star would stab him to his heart. He eyed the other decorations; designer, like the ones Cadence might have chosen. Those he could handle, but the star took him back to a much happier place and time. It didn't match the other ornaments and the crisp cranberry and popcorn garlands. The pink and silver star didn't fit in with the red and gold.

Matt slumped into the recliner and wrestled with the emotions brewing at the front of his eyes, choking his throat, and battling for his nose.

Joie stepped through the swinging doors from the kitchen, side-stepping the mistletoe. Warmth momentarily pushed away his gloomy mood thinking about the kiss they'd shared.

"Hi, did you have a nice time with Dawnetta?" Joie's mention of Miss Hall's first name sounded forced.

"It was nice."

"That's good." Joie swallowed.

Matt glanced back at the star. "Where did you find the tree topper?"

"I, uh...." She hesitated, pinching her lips together. He could tell she was working on not telling a factlet.

"Just tell me the truth. It's a lot easier than you trying to figure out how to get around a lie."

Joie wrinkled her nose, the corner of her mouth turned up in a half smile. Adorable. He liked her face when she tried to skirt the truth. "Oh, gumdrops, fine. Wink put it up there. He did most of the decorating since he still has his magic." Her eyes dropped to the floor. "I hope you don't mind."

Matt rose from the recliner and crossed to Joie. "Your friend, Wink, he did a nice thing for me."

"He did?" Joie's gaze shot from the floor to Matt's face.

"That was the star Cadence and I picked out on our first Christmas." He wanted to take her hand, pull her under the mistletoe as an excuse to kiss her again, had to know if the sensations he had for her right now were real.

Joie pulled away from his touch. "Emily and I made gingerbread cookies. She's decorating them. Want to come see?" She returned to the kitchen passing hastily under the mistletoe.

He dropped his hand to his side. "They smell delicious." Matt followed Joie into the kitchen, lingering for a moment to see if Joie noticed he stood under the mistletoe. She didn't, or pretended she didn't.

"Look, Daddy." Emily held up one of her creations. "He looks like you."

Matt took the cookie. Sure enough, the little man sported a glob of yellow frosting that must have represented a hard hat. A brown smear across the waist formed a tool belt, complete with different colors that were his tools, and brown boots adorned the feet. "Perfect."

"I did it all by myself." She grinned. "Aren't you going to eat it?"

He didn't want to disappoint his daughter, so he took a nibble off the foot, the flavors delectable on his tongue. "Delicious." He gave a scrumptious sigh.

"Joie made them. I just frosted them." She motioned to where the countertop lay strewn with gingerbread men as if marshalled in military ranks.

Matt did a quick calculation. "I don't think we'll need that many for the Christmas party."

"I know that." Joie didn't meet his gaze. "I'm going to take some to the group home for the teens there. And I thought Santa might need a few extra for the kids in the orphanage in Brazil."

"That's really nice of you." Although, he realized that that many cookies wouldn't be nearly enough.

As if reading his thoughts, she said, "Oh, Mrs. Claus has magic that can multiply them."

Joie had said that the Claus's ran the North Pole together. He just hoped that one of them would find the perfect solution when she returned home. Once she was back where she belonged, Joie would probably never give him another thought. Matt knew he'd be thinking about Joie for a very long time; probably the rest of his life.

CHAPTER THIRTY-SEVEN

Matt stood beside the refreshment table with Dawnetta at his side. Joie had decided to come, along with his mother, Emily and Ethan. With a wrinkle of his nose, he hoped Ethan wouldn't try to schmooze Joie. He'd always been a lady's man. In high school, he'd had no end of girlfriends and wannabes.

"You have to try my cookies." Dawnetta had already filled her plate with delectable goodies of different varieties. She placed a sugar cookie shaped like a tree and covered in green frosting on his plate.

He picked it up. It looked pretty good. Smelled delicious. The overpowering taste of sugar flooded his mouth. He sighed, looking for a drink. There was more to a woman than her cooking.

"That good, huh?" She must have taken his sigh as one of delight.

"They're yummy." A factlet. That's what some women wanted to hear. It was easier than the truth.

She linked her arm in his and guided him across the room. "Thanks so much for asking me to the party. It helps me forget my fiancé."

"I'm sorry about that."

Dawnetta smiled, but he could tell it was a fake one, trying a bit too hard to not think about the man she was probably still pining over.

"I really miss him. I hope you understand." She stopped at a table near the back of the room.

Matt pulled out a chair for her. "Of course, I do." It had been two years since Cadence's accident, and Matt still ached for his wife.

One of the church members pointed over their heads. "Oh, look, there's mistletoe right above you."

Matt cleared his throat, and color flushed up on Dawnetta's face.

"Go on, then, kiss her, you fool."

Dawnetta glanced up at Matt.

Matt's throat went dry. He'd heard that after one kiss a person could tell whether or not they were compatible. A simple kiss could ignite the passion or....

He stood, held out his hand inviting her to join him.

Dawnetta's blush deepened.

He leaned in, but kept his body from touching hers. Someone behind them clapped and called out. "Go get 'er, Matt."

Dawnetta chuckled – a nervous, high-pitched giggle. She closed her eyes and tilted her face up.

Matt lowered his head, barely grazing her lips with his. He did not close his eyes, but looked to see who was watching them. His mother pushed Emily into the room followed by Ethan, his mouth open in surprise. Hustling directly toward them, he yanked Matt away from Dawnetta. "What are you doing kissing my fiancé?"

"You're her fiancé?"

"Ethan!" Dawnetta squealed and threw her arms around his neck.

"What the..." Matt almost swore, but remembered it might not be appropriate in a church.

The people around his table, who'd been watching the open display of affection chittered, some in shock, some in amusement, some clearly looking for something to gossip about.

The look on his daughter's face showed her displeasure. She certainly didn't resemble the angel she was supposed to display in the nativity. His mother's face mirrored the same un-angelic look as his daughter.

Joie stood beside his mother. Confusion crinkled her nose and shot from her eyes. "What?" She mouthed to him from across the room.

Matt strode past Emily and headed straight to Joie, but stopped short when he spotted – Laura Milo with the man from the Christmas tree lot and two boys who looked like they belonged together. "What are you doing here?"

"We were invited..." Laura turned back to Joie.

Grabbing Joie's arm, he pulled her out into the hallway. "Why is Laura Milo here?" Matt turned loose of her, his fists clenching and unclenching.

"And her husband and their two sons. We invited them to come." Joie's expression turned to confusion. "Did I do something wrong?"

"Yes, Joie, you did. Big time." Matt couldn't believe that Joie would do that without asking him first how he felt about it.

"I thought it would be a nice opportunity for you to hear her apologize. She's written you several times and – "

Matt cut her off. "I've never gotten a single letter saying "I'm sorry."

"That's because she was too scared to mail them."

"You have meddled for the last time." He paced back and forth muttering. "Go home, Joie. Go back to where you won't be causing any more problems. Go home, back to the North Pole."

Matt didn't wait for her reply, instead, he turned his back on her and strode out of the party and got into his truck. Revving the engine, he peeled out of the parking lot and shot down the lonely lane into the darkness. Anger boiled up in him. All he was trying to do was to make his daughter happy. He'd just lost Dawnetta, apparently he never really had her. But at least he liked her. Emily liked her. It would have been an okay match. He swore at Ethan under his breath.

He really didn't even want a wife. That elf should have never showed up. All she had done was cause trouble. He swore. It didn't help that he'd developed feelings for her.

Once he'd reached the cemetery, he stayed in his car, the headlights beaming on his wife's headstone. "Why, God, why her? There are so many other people you could have taken, why my wife? Why not Laura Milo?"

He rested his head against the steering wheel for so long his head pounded at his temples. When he finally lifted his head, he stared out at the gray stone with his wife's name and dates and that little dash between that was supposed to represent her entire life. The flowers resting on the ground still looked fresh like someone had recently put them there. Today was the anniversary of her death. He should have brought his daughter here. The flowers had to be from his mother.

Matt got out of his truck and tromped through the wet grass. Phlox and roses. Cadence's favorite. Yes, definitely the work of his mother. Stifling a sob, he picked them up and brought them to his nose. One of the thorns pricked his thumb. He growled and bent to lay the flowers down. A snow globe sat where the flowers had been.

He picked it up and turned it over in his hands. The snow swirled around the bust of a woman. When the white mist inside settled, a likeness of Cadence appeared. Her smile beamed up at him, while a soft hymn played, one he didn't want to hear. Love, forgiveness, and God's mercy.

"Who put this here?" He turned it over in his hands for a clue.

"I did." A woman appeared, her red dress fringed in white fur reached her knees. Black boots with gold buckles adorned her feet. Her brown hair hung softly around her beautiful, round face.

"I thought angels dressed in white."

Her smile lit her face giving her a resplendent glow, or perhaps it was merely the beam of his headlights. Matt rubbed his eyes.

"Angels come in all forms. Most of them are those around us who are neighbors, friends, and an occasional elf." Her eyes twinkled.

"Are *you* Mrs. Claus?" Matt took a step back. After all that had happened, he really shouldn't be surprised.

"In the flesh." A warm giggle surrounded him.

"Why are you here?"

Mrs. Claus chuckled. "A little girl sent me a letter. She needs a father whose heart will heal and move on." She took the globe from Matt, wound the key on the bottom replaying the hymn, then she gave it a quick shake, sending the white flakes swirling around Cadence while the music filled the air.

"I'll never get over Cadence's death." The grief welled up inside him.

"No, of course not. But the bitterness you are feeling can turn to peace, if you will simply forgive." Mrs. Claus handed the globe back to Matt.

Matt held it, staring at Cadence's image. When he looked up, Mrs. Claus smiled at him and gazed directly into his eyes. "I was going to wait and give it to you on Christmas Eve. But it looks like you might need it a day earlier." Little crows' feet appeared at the corners of her eyes when she smiled.

He shook the globe again and watched the flakes flutter inside. "Where did you get this?" he asked and found himself standing alone at Cadence's grave.

CHAPTER THIRTY-EIGHT

Too late to return to the party, Matt headed home, then sat in the driveway for a long time trying to process what had just happened. Had he really talked to Mrs. Claus? He picked up the snow globe and wound the key on the bottom. Nothing happened. Maybe he'd wound it too tight. Yet, every time he shook the globe, his wife smiled back at him like some sort of magic hologram.

The rain started again. His mother and daughter had probably long since gone home. He'd missed his daughter's performance as an angel. Ethan and Dawnetta had probably found a ride home. At least someone was happy tonight.

Matt set the globe on the seat next to him. The haunting melody suddenly filled the truck. Fluky thing. He picked it up and tucked it under his arm, got out of his truck, and ran toward the house. The rain from the gutter dripped onto his head and ran down his back. He should have cleaned that out when the oak started shedding her leaves.

Once he entered the house, he noticed the Christmas tree lights were off and the room was almost dark. His mother sat under the light of a table lamp reading her Good Book.

She looked up and frowned. "I have no idea what possessed you to act like such a clod." She didn't even wait for him to say anything. "First, you kissed another man's fiancée in front of the whole congregation. Emily is devastated, by the way. She thought Miss Hall was going to be her new mother."

"About that..."

"Yes, about that. Whose fool-brained idea was that?" She closed the Bible and set it on the table.

"I had no idea Ethan was her fiancé." Matt couldn't believe his mother was actually suggesting he'd planned that.

"And then that horrible snub of Laura Milo." Mom shook her head. "We're supposed to welcome folks to church, no matter what they did."

"Joie had no business inviting them without clearing it with me first." Matt ran his hand along the back of his neck.

"Joie didn't invite them. Emily did." Her angry mom-gaze pierced him through.

"But Joie said she invited them." No that wasn't quite right. "I mean she said we."

"It was a collective we." Mom shook her head. "We went to Cadence's grave to put her favorite flowers at her headstone. Laura was there."

"What was she doing there?" Matt couldn't imagine why the woman would want to visit Cadence, especially killing her as she did.

"It looked like she was grieving." Mom stood up and crossed to him, then put her hand on his shoulder. "You know, you're not the only one who is grieving."

Matt hung his head and stepped away from his mother. His mother was right, he should not have acted as he did. "What happened to their family after I left? Did they stay?"

Mom shook her head. "No, you pretty much ruined their night. Laura busted up crying. Her husband guided her out of the building.

I didn't quite hear what he said, but I'm pretty sure they'll never set foot inside our church again.

Matt couldn't stand how dark the room suddenly felt. He reached down and plugged in the tree. The room lit with enough brilliance to chase away any gloom, except the blackness in his soul. Joie had added such beautiful touches to the house. He should tell her he was sorry for his accusation. Matt glanced down the hall. "Is Joie putting Emily to bed?"

"Nobody could find her after you left." Mom straightened a garland not quite in line with the others. "What did you say to her?"

Matt hung his head. He'd been so angry at her, thinking she was the one who'd invited Laura. "I told her to go home."

"Then I guess that's what she did."

CHAPTER THIRTY-NINE

Joie lay with her head on Mrs. Claus's knee and sobbed. "I've failed. Everything is ruined. Matt will never find a wife and Emily will never get a mother."

Mrs. Claus stroked Joie's hair. "It's never as gloomy as you think it is."

"Yes, it is." Joie raised her head to look into Mrs. Claus's eyes. "I nearly got him killed when he ran after Miss Hall's tire. I set his kitchen on fire. Then I had to use all three miracles to put it out and not get him in trouble for leaving two children home alone." The tears refused to stop running down her cheeks.

Mrs. Claus took a handkerchief from out of the air and dabbed Joie's face. "Things are not entirely as they seem."

"And now I've lost the opportunity to head the Bright Twinkle department." Joie took the hankie and blew her nose and wailed even louder. She hated her human body. Things felt ten...no a hundred times worse than an elf. "And I've done the worst thing ever. I fell in love with my client." Joie dropped onto the rug and curled into a ball.

Mrs. Claus stood and went to her tintinnabulum and gave it a tug. "Send Wink Everwarmth immediately."

"I don't want to see him." Joie rolled over and buried her face in her hands. "Just send me to the coal mine. It's no less than I deserve."

With a strength Joie didn't know Mrs. Claus had, she yanked her off the floor and plopped her on the couch. "We can't have Wink seeing you disgrace yourself."

Wink came through the study door. "You called, Mrs. Claus?"

Mrs. Claus drifted across the room and motioned for Wink to sit next to Joie on the sofa. She then lowered a projection screen. "My dear, you are not the failure you seem to think you are." Her gaze turned to a glower directed at Wink. "Let's see exactly what was going on."

She punched a few buttons on the console at her desk. "Now then, you see how you so effortlessly pushed the tire so that it rolled down the slope. And look, there's Matthew Adams chasing after it, followed by Miss Dawnetta Hall. Matt stopped. Oh, and look, Dawnetta stopped. But Wink..."

Joie gasped when Wink pushed Dawnetta into Matt, sending him into oncoming traffic.

Wink stuttered. "I didn't mean to push her that hard. I was only trying to get them closer together."

"Uh, huh." Mrs. Claus raised one eyebrow. "And the papers in the kitchen? How do you explain that?" She pressed a few more buttons.

Joie covered her eyes. She did not want to see Matt's kitchen go up in flames again.

Mrs. Claus gave her arm a light tap. "You'll want to see this."

Next to her, Wink squirmed. "Don't get excited. It was an accident."

"Uh, huh." Mrs. Claus raised the other eyebrow.

Joie had her back to the stove, taking the cookies off the pan. Behind her the knob on the stovetop turned and glowed red. Several papers slid across the counter and rested on the burner. Poof, they shot up in flames.

Joie's eyes widened. "Wink?"

"That's right. Wink." Mrs. Claus shut the video off.

"But Mrs. Claus, I used the miracles." Joie knew those were her fault.

"That's true." Wink agreed.

A smirk crossed Mrs. Claus's face. "If you hadn't set the house on fire, Joie wouldn't have used those miracles. They were not used on herself because she wanted to be a human...." Mrs. Claus placed her fingers under Joie's chin and smiled affectionately. "She used them to keep Matthew Adams's house from being burned to the ground and keeping him out of jail because of child neglect and endangerment."

"But, but...," Wink stammered.

"Oh, and how about the star on top of the tree to upset Matthew? Or at the Christmas party – the mistletoe, Ethan showing up at just the right time?" Mrs. Claus went back to the projection screen.

"What about Laura Milo at the cemetery?" Joie asked.

Wink jumped off the couch. "I had nothing to do with that."

"No, of course you didn't." Mrs. Claus's smirk turned to a frown. "That's why I'm only giving you three months in the coal mine.

"Three months? I don't deserve that. I was next in line for head of Bright Twinkle," Wink huffed and paced the floor.

"Why would you do that to me?" Joie stood and towered over Wink. "You were never in love with me, were you?"

Mrs. Claus shook her finger. "No factlets, Wink."

"I knew if you failed, you'd never be made head of Bright Twinkle." Wink stared at his shoes.

"You did all that because you wanted that position." Joie slumped to the couch. "All you had to do was ask. I would have gladly stepped aside. I was quite happy in the Woods and Wheels division."

Mrs. Claus put a heavy hand on Wink's shoulder and led him to the door. "I suppose you will have a lot to think about in the next three months. But first, Santa has a special job for you to do. Brundle is out with a nasty cold."

Joie couldn't help but snicker. Pooper scooper supreme, the head elf who got to ride with Santa on Christmas Eve and make sure none of the reindeer left anything behind.

Wink gave a deep growl and stomped out of the study, slamming the door behind him.

Mrs. Claus turned back to Joie. "You did admirably well. The position is still yours if you want it." A bright smile flowed across her whole being as she pointed to the remaining charm on Joie's bracelet. "All you need to do is use that last miracle and change back into an elf. Or is there something else you desire?"

CHAPTER FORTY

Matt knew it was late. He didn't care. There was something he had to do before the night ended. He zipped his coat up and headed for the door. "Will you keep an eye on Emily?"

His mother still stood beside the tree fingering the ornaments. "Where are you going?"

"I have to ask for forgiveness." He didn't wait for his mother to respond, but left the house and got into his truck. Then searching his phone, he tracked down the Milo family living in the next town over.

What a hard-hearted fool he'd been. He'd been so wrapped up in his own grief, he'd failed to recognize his was not the only loss. Laura had not only been leaning heavily on her husband, but on a cane as well. The young man, too had a saddened countenance. Guilt weighed heavier than grief.

He pulled into the driveway. The house was dark, except for a light shining through the garage windows.

Matt got out of his truck and could hear the motor of a car running inside. He walked up to the door and banged on it, bringing no response. Panic set in. If someone was inside, they could be in trouble. His cousin had died that way, drunk and clearly not thinking, he'd passed out with the car parked in the garage. Forensics officers said that it had only taken forty-five minutes for him to die.

Banging again in earnest, he shouted. "Open the door. You're going to die." Still no response.

Matt ran to the front door and rang the bell, followed by pounding.

Mr. Milo answered the door. Once he saw Matt, he tried to slam it in his face.

Matthew pushed the door open, nearly knocking Mr. Milo to the ground.

"What do you think you're doing here? Haven't you hurt us enough for one night?" Mr. Milo shoved Matt back onto the sidewalk and shut the door.

"Wait!" Matt hollered against the wood. "Is someone in the garage? There's a car running." He kept banging on the door. When no one answered he dialed 9-1-1. "Please, help me."

Before he could explain to dispatch his emergency, the garage door opened and Mr. Milo carried Laura to the wet lawn and laid her on it.

Their two sons had followed their father and now knelt in the grass.

"Please, Mama, wake up." The youngest one held her hand and patted it.

"I know CPR." Matt handed his phone to Mr. Milo. "It's 9-1-1. Tell them what's going on." He began trying to resuscitate Laura.

Mr. Milo took the phone. Matt didn't pay attention to his conversation, but kept doing chest compressions. "Please breathe," he said between his mouth-to-mouth breaths.

In what seemed like an eternity, the wail of sirens pierced the misty night. Paramedics took over.

Mr. Milo stood with his hands clasped in prayer, while the boys cried.

Matt knelt on the ground. He paused, looking up into the face of Laura's husband; the anguish filling his eyes, the tears streaming down his face pierced Matt's heart. If anyone understood what it meant to lose a wife, Matt did.

The boys held onto each other, their pleas for their mother twisted in his chest. How could he have wished Laura dead? "Please God; don't take her from this sweet family. It's okay that my Cadence is gone, but please, let her live. Let her live. They need her..." A sob of his own rent his heart. "I need to ask her to forgive me."

Matt sobbed, no longer the tears of bitterness, but tears of forgiveness washed over him.

A hand touched his shoulder. Matt looked up into the eyes of one of the paramedics. "She's going to be okay."

CHAPTER FORTY-ONE

Mrs. Claus put her hands on Joie's shoulders and turned her to face the mirror. "You make such a wonderful human; it's almost a shame to turn you back into an elf."

Joie stared at her reflection. "You'd still let me have the supervisory position at Bright Twinkle?"

"You're the best elf for the job." Mrs. Claus touched the last charm on Joie's bracelet. "All you have to do is make the miracle happen and become an elf again. You can have any position in North Pole Kingdom. You've even proven yourself enough that you can ride in Santa's sleigh and help deliver presents tonight."

That was the greatest honor bestowed on any elf. Joie nodded, but her heart beat almost four thousand miles away with a sweet little girl and her father. She sighed and willed the tears back. He'd commanded her to go home and stop meddling. She took one last look in the mirror. "I'm ready to be an elf again."

Mrs. Claus put her hand to Joie's cheek. "You can stay a human if you want. You're not the first elf to want to remain a human after changing into one."

"What's the point if Matt doesn't want me?" Her heart seized for a moment. Maybe it was for the best to go back to being an elf. "I'll be the best helper in all of North Pole Kingdom."

"You're sure that's what you want?" Mrs. Claus removed the charm and placed it in Joie's hand.

Joie closed her hand around the tiny charm shaped like a gingerbread man, complete with a yellow hard hat and tool belt. Those miracles had gotten her into trouble in the first place. When she turned back into an elf, she would forget how much she loved Matt. Joie wanted to hang onto those feelings for him for one more night. "Do I have to be an elf to ride with Santa?"

"I don't think there's a rule against it. But you'd probably need to check with Santa."

As if on cue, Kris entered waving a piece of paper and definitely not sounding so jolly. "What is this?"

Mrs. Claus took the sheet from him and read it over. "How did you get this?" Before Santa could respond, she answered her own question. "Oh; Wink gave this to you?"

"Yes, and I hear things didn't go very well." He stopped when he spied Joie. "Who is that?"

"That is your new sleigh assistant for tonight and the new supervisor for Bright Twinkle lighting division."

"Joie?" Santa stepped in front of her and stared into her eyes. "How did you end up like this?"

It was one thing to have to explain it to Mrs. Claus, but Santa? "I _"

"Used her miracles in the most benevolent manner," Mrs. Claus interceded. "And I'll have you to know it was Wink's meddling that made her mission a near disaster. So don't you dare go blaming Joie for any of this."

Santa's face softened. "Laila, how many times have we discussed not trying to fulfill Christmas wishes that we can't create right within our workshops?"

"I know." She snuggled against his chest and gazed all starry-eyed up at him. "You read the letter. How could I turn down such a request?"

"You have the softest heart." He reached into his bag and pulled a golden retriever from its depths. "I believe Emily also asked for a puppy. I'm sure she'll be surprised tomorrow morning when she sees him sitting under the tree."

Joie took the wiggling ball of fur and cuddled him under her chin. "He looks just like the one in the picture in Emily's room. She's going to love him."

Santa retrieved the puppy and put him back in the bag. "You better hurry and get ready if you're going to come with me. You'll never be warm enough in those clothes."

After he left, Mrs. Claus waved a miracle over Joie's head and dressed her in elf clothes once more. She fastened her bracelet around her wrist. "You probably won't need it, but just in case, you can still use it to get home."

"Thanks, Mrs. Claus." Joie wrapped her arms around Mrs. Claus.

"Tonight while you are out helping Santa, you be thinking about that miracle. The choice is yours."

CHAPTER FORTY-TWO

Emily hollered from her bed downstairs. "Daddy! It's Christmas. Come get me up. I want to see what Santa left."

Weary, Matt trudged down the stairs. "It's not even six o'clock. Can't I sleep for one more hour?"

She struggled to prop herself into a sitting position. "No! I didn't get a mommy for Christmas, so Santa better have left me something amazing, or I'm never writing to him again."

"All right." Matt lifted her into her wheelchair and pushed her into the living room. The lights from the tree burned bright, shining on a few packages underneath. "Let me go wake up your grandmother." He turned to head back up the stairs then stopped. "Don't touch anything until I get Grandma down here."

"But, Daddy, that box is moving." Emily rolled closer to the tree.

"Don't open it," he warned her before he headed up the stairs. Knocking softly on the guest bedroom door, he called. "Mom, Emily's awake. Christmas won't wait."

The door sprung open. "Oh, goodie! I love Christmas morning." She flashed past him and bounded down the stairs with all the glee of a child.

Matt shook his head. "Don't start without me."

Once he reached the living room, Emily sat with a yellow puppy on her lap. The box and ribbon lay at her feet. "Look what Santa brought me!" She giggled at the wriggling mass of fur as it licked her face and nipped at her chin.

"Mom, you shouldn't have done that without consulting me first." Matt had no idea how he was going to find the time to train a dog.

Mom looked as surprised as he felt. "It wasn't me."

"Sillies, it was Santa." Emily hugged the puppy so hard she might choke it. "Since he didn't get me a new mommy, the least he could do was bring me a dog."

Mom raised her eyebrows. "She has a point."

Matt sighed gruffly.

Mom picked up a small box and handed it to Matt. "It looks like Santa left something for you, too."

He peeled the ribbon off and lifted the snow globe Mrs. Claus had given him the night of the party. No wonder he couldn't find it. She'd taken it back and rewrapped it. That was kind of lame. Then again, he really hadn't wanted anything for Christmas except for his daughter to be happy.

Matt gave it a shake, the white images obscuring his deceased wife's image.

"That's really pretty," Mom said. "Is that Cadence?"

Matt nodded, then turned it over and wound the key. Instead of the hymn he'd heard the night before, it played "God Rest Ye Merry Gentlemen." In his mind he heard the words, "It's time to find Joie," just as the song played "oh oh, tidings of comfort and joy...comfort and joy."

Cadence smile at him. "Matt, it's time for you to find joy."

Her image changed and was replaced by a clear picture of Joie. "I love you."

His heart leapt to his throat. How was this even possible? "Where are you?"

The globe went blank. His heart that had been beating in his chest, now plummeted to his feet.

"What's wrong?" his mom asked, taking the snow globe from him and shaking it. "Hey, it's Joie."

The doorbell rang. Matt sprang to his feet and raced to open it. He just knew Joie waited on the other side.

Instead, a man dressed as Santa stood on his porch. "I have one more gift for you."

Dumbfounded, Matt couldn't speak, but eyed the man.

Santa didn't wait for his reply. "You see, some miracles can't be explained. Some are brushed off as mere coincidence. The most precious are the ones we never expect."

Joie stepped from behind Santa. "I promise I'll be the best mommy for Emily."

Matt choked back the lump of happiness forming in his throat.

"If you'll have me." She fluttered her eyelashes.

"Of course, I will." Matt gathered Joie to him; his arms wrapped around her, and he buried his face in her hair. Even though the chilly air blew past him, warmth shot through his whole body, feeling the closeness of her. His lips found hers pressing lightly at first and growing more intense. Her hands linked around the back of his neck.

Matt had no idea how long he reveled in the joy of her until Santa cleared his throat. "I think my deliveries are done."

Matt released Joie and they turned to face Santa.

Joie held out the gingerbread man charm to Santa. "I don't think I'll be needing this."

Santa didn't take it, but wrapped her fingers around the charm. "Matt is your final miracle. Keep it on your bracelet."

Joie kissed Santa on his cheek. "I will miss you."

Santa wrapped her in a hug and looked over her shoulder at Matt. "You're one lucky man to find such a joy. My work is done, and now I need a long winter's nap."

Emily clapped her hands in delight. "Thank you Santa for a new mommy and a puppy."

His mother stood with her mouth hanging open, then she smiled. "I guess I shouldn't be so surprised. See, I knew you should have been dating Joie all along."

With a smile lighting his face and a twinkle in his eye, Santa said, "Mrs. Claus may run North Pole Kingdom, but I get to deliver the best gifts."

About the Author

Betsy Love has loved to write from the moment she could hold a pen and has been creating stories ever since she was in elementary school. Her high school creative writing teacher told her that one day she would be published.

When not sitting at her computer pouring her heart and soul into her novels, she loves going to their mountain property for inspiration and to escape the desert heat. She loves spending time with her family. At last count she has 20 grandchildren, has given up on gardening. If she had a horse, she might give up writing.

ACKNOWLEDGMENTS

DeWalt, always. He is my biggest fan and sounding board. And some days he annoys the crud out of me when he asks, "Is that all you wrote today?"

DeAnna Browne for suggested changes to make it the best book it could be. Never mind that she bled all over the pages.

Anne Marie Jenner and her love for everything I write, and believing in me.

Stephanie Nelson, Gussie Fick, and Ann Hunter for their encouragement.

Sarah Waggoner, my incredibly talented daughter for the beautiful cover! I'm not prejudiced at all.

BOOKS BY BETSY LOVE

SweetHart's Café Series

An Unexpected Miracle

An Unexpected Blessing

Mail Order StarBrides series

The Healer's Heart

Falling for a Fraud

Surrogate Hearts

The Gravity of a Kiss

The Matchmaker's Match

Losing Grace-A Christmas Time Travel

Plotting for Pantsers in 6 Easy Steps

Identity-*Out of Print*

Soulfire-*Out of Print*

Young Adult Books by Lizzie Anne Love

Mystic's Tale Series
The Dragon Keeper
The Dragon Keeper's Destiny
Coming soon: The Dragon's Realm

The Penny Project

If you loved this book, please leave a review!

Sign up for my newsletter at www.betsylove.com and receive updates on new releases and free stories you'll love!

CONNECT WITH ME ONLINE:

Website: www.electric-scroll.com
Blog: BetsyLove.com
Email: authorbetsylove@gmail.com
Facebook: Betsy Love LDS Author
Twitter: @BetsyLoveAuthor
Google+: BetsyLove

Made in the USA
Columbia, SC
25 June 2022